Anonymous

Proceedings at a Banquet Given by his Friends to the Hon.

Marshall Pinckney Wilder, PH. D.

on his birthday, September 22, 1883, to commemorate the completion of

his eighty-fifth year

Anonymous

Proceedings at a Banquet Given by his Friends to the Hon. Marshall Pinckney Wilder, PH. D.
on his birthday, September 22, 1883, to commemorate the completion of his eighty-fifth year

ISBN/EAN: 9783337381493

Printed in Europe, USA, Canada, Australia, Japan

Cover: Foto ©Andreas Hilbeck / pixelio.de

More available books at **www.hansebooks.com**

PROCEEDINGS

AT A

BANQUET GIVEN BY HIS FRIENDS

TO THE

Hon. MARSHALL PINCKNEY WILDER, Ph.D.

On his Birthday, September 22, 1883,

TO COMMEMORATE THE

COMPLETION OF HIS EIGHTY-FIFTH YEAR.

Serus in cœlum redeas, diuque
Lætus intersis populo.

HORACE: Lib. 1. Car. 2.

CAMBRIDGE:

UNIVERSITY PRESS.

1883.

TABLE OF CONTENTS.

BANQUET

HON. MARSHALL P. WILDER.

On the twenty-second day of September, 1883, the Hon. MARSHALL P. WILDER completed the eighty-fifth year of his age. A short time previous, a few of his friends, members of the Massachusetts Horticultural Society, desiring to testify their appreciation of his services to that association, and to other institutions with which he had been connected, conceived the idea of tendering to him a banquet to commemorate his birthday. A Committee, consisting of Messrs. CHARLES H. B. BRECK, ROBERT MANNING, and JOHN C. HOVEY sent out invitations to the personal friends of Mr. Wilder, belonging to the various institutions in which he is interested, to join them in tendering to him the honor of a dinner at the Parker House, in Boston. The idea, so appropriately conceived, was admirably carried

out.   More than a hundred gentlemen were present
on the occasion, most of whom had occupied high
positions in the State and Nation, and in the walks
of learning and letters.

The dining-hall, under the direction of Mr. Joseph
H. Beckman, one of the proprietors of the Parker
House, was fitly ornamented with the richest trophies
of the flower-garden, arranged with exquisite taste.
These decorations of floral beauty, filling twenty
magnificent baskets, gifts from Messrs. H. H. Hunnewell, Francis B. Hayes, John L. Gardner, the
Messrs. Hovey and Company, and Mrs. E. S. Joyce,
were the delight and admiration of the party.   Mrs.
Joyce, of Medford, contributed also a bouquet of
exquisite and crowning beauty.   At the upper end
of the hall were two fine specimens of the Victoria
Regia, and other lilies, presented by E. S. Sturde-
vant, of New Jersey.   Most agreeable music was
discoursed by the Germania Band.   On the cover of
the *Menu* was a splendid life-like portrait of Colonel
Wilder, and by the side of each plate was placed a
Grace-Wilder carnation pink, relieved by maiden-hair
fern, making an exquisite *boutonnière*.   This carnation is a seedling raised by Mr. Joseph Tailby, of
Wellesley, and was named by him for a daughter
of Colonel Wilder, in honor of her father.

Mr. Charles H. B. Breck, chairman of the Committee, presided.   The Hon. Francis M. Weld,

Vice-President of the Massachusetts Agricultural Club, occupied the head of one of the tables, and Benjamin G. Smith, Esq., Vice-President of the Massachusetts Horticultural Society, presided at the other. Colonel WILDER, whose entrance was greeted with prolonged applause, occupied the seat of honor.

The venerable GEORGE W. BLAGDEN, D.D., at the request of the President, invoked a blessing in the following words : —

OUR FATHER who art in heaven, we worship Thee as the God of whom it is declared in Thy Word that " There is one Lawgiver." Thou hast ordained, and dost continually uphold in their operation, those laws of nature and of providence in the workings of which, as we obey and use them, Thou givest us, day by day, our daily bread. Thou hast thus left not Thyself without a witness, in "that Thou hast done good, and given us rain from heaven, and fruitful seasons, filling our hearts with food and gladness." And Thou hast assured us that every creature of Thine is good, and nothing to be refused if it be received with thanksgiving, and is sanctified by Thy word, and by prayer. Help us, now, to receive Thy gifts before us with thanksgiving, and to sanctify them by Thy word and by prayer.

May Thy servant, whose birthday and ripened age we now commemorate, and who, in studying and obeying Thy natural and providential laws, has been so extensively Thine instrument in filling the hearts of his fellow-men with food and gladness, be also, through Thy grace, so obedient to Thine eternal law of love, in the penitence, faith, and obedience of Thy gospel, as to " have fruit unto holiness, and the end thereof be everlasting life" to his soul, through Jesus Christ our Lord, to whom be glory forever. Amen.

At the conclusion of the dinner, the President, the Hon. Mr. BRECK, spoke as follows: —

GENTLEMEN, — The occasion which brings us together this evening is of great interest to us all. We come here to offer our congratulations to, and to express the sentiments of love and admiration which we feel for, the oldest merchant of the city of Boston, on this the eighty-fifth anniversary of his birth. For more than fifty years he has been a director in the Hamilton Bank, and for forty years a director in the New England Life Insurance Company. He is the father of the Massachusetts Agricultural College and of the State Board of Agriculture. He was the founder and President of the United States Agricultural Society. His influence has been felt throughout the country. For a third of a century he has held the important office of President of the American Pomological Society, whose members are found in every State of the Union, and also in the Dominion of Canada. He was one of the founders of the Massachusetts Institute of Technology, was for many years a vice-president, and the chairman of its Society of Arts. From its organization he has been a director. He is President of the Massachusetts Agricultural Club, now in the forty-fourth year of its existence. For twenty years he was President of the Norfolk County Agricultural Society, and for eight years President of the Massachusetts Horticultural Society. For sixteen years he has been President of the New England Historic Genealogical Society. He has also been active in founding and in aiding other societies. He is the oldest living ex-president of the Massachusetts Senate, and also the oldest ex-commander of the Ancient and Honorable Artillery Company. But I will not continue to enumerate the many important positions of trust which he has held with honor to himself and benefit to his countrymen. I give you as my sentiment, THE HEALTH, PROLONGED LIFE, AND CONTINUED USEFULNESS OF OUR WELCOME GUEST, THE HON. MARSHALL PINCKNEY WILDER.

Colonel WILDER responded in a clear and distinct voice, as follows : —

MY FRIENDS, — Language is too feeble to express the gratitude I feel for the generous ovation with which you are crowning the anniversary of my birth. Mr. President, could I believe that I was worthy of the praise which you have so kindly bestowed upon me, I should feel that my mission on earth was nearly ended, and that I was about ready to be gathered to my fathers, like a shock of corn fully ripe in its season. But no, no; although I am somewhat advanced in years, I do not feel that my work is done. Before I go home, I have something more to do for those great interests to which I have given so much of my life. You have spoken of my connection with various institutions and callings, and I thank you for remembering me as an old merchant of Boston, for it is from this vocation that I have derived the means to aid these other interests. Yes, I am an old merchant ; I have been constantly in business for nearly threescore years in this city, and I beg to assure you, my friends, that there is no title which I prize more highly than that of an upright, intelligent, and enterprising merchant of Boston.

It is our good fortune, my friends, to live in an age of remarkable progress and activity; in a nation whose growth, prosperity, and power are the wonder and admiration of the world. Much of this progress I have witnessed in my own day. At the time of my birth the population of this nation was only about five millions; now it is more than fifty millions. When I came to this city there was not a mile of railroad on this continent; now there are 120,000 miles. And let us never forget that it was by the bold enterprise of one of our own citizens that the first great railroad was opened across it to the Pacific shores. All honor to the memory of Oakes Ames and to his worthy associates! And let us also remember how much we are indebted to Benjamin P. Cheney and his associates for the completion of that great northern road, opening another thoroughfare for Europe and Asia, and for the development of the immense resources of the great Northwest of America.

Mr. President, you have referred to me in connection with those industrial interests on which depend, more than on any other, the prosperity and happiness of the world. It is true I have done something for these, believing that I could do nothing better for my fellow-men. At the time of my birth there were not half a dozen agricultural societies, and for nearly a quarter of a century after-

ward not a single horticultural society, in our land;
now there are more than fifteen hundred of these
and similar associations recorded in the Department
of Agriculture at Washington. Then the products
of our soil were not deemed worthy of a place in the
statistics of our nation; now we produce more than
two billions of bushels of grain, with a constant reserve sufficient to supply the deficiency of the Old
World. When I came to this city no steamship had
ever reached our shores; now there is not a day in
the year when many of them do not enter or depart
from our ports. But I need not prolong this strain
of remark. Suffice it to say that, in science, art, and
civilization, and in everything that pertains to the
comfort and happiness of mankind, the present age
is transcendently superior to any that has preceded it.
When I review the past history of our country and
look forward to its future greatness and glory, my soul
yearns for another fourscore and five years, that I
may see its two hundred millions of happy freemen
rejoicing in the blessings of liberty, peace, and union,
all united in one great circle of life and love; one
in interest, one in destiny, one in a glorious union,
never to be broken, —

> "The union of lakes, the union of lands,
> The union of States none can sever;
> The union of hearts, the union of hands,
> And the Flag of our Union forever!"

And now, my friends, in closing these remarks, permit me again to say, I thank you from the bottom of my heart for this kind demonstration of your friendship and regard. May the choicest of Heaven's blessings descend and rest on you through life; and when we shall have passed over to that better land not far away, if any of you shall come where I am, you will be received with open arms and a thankful heart, as a token of my appreciation of the honor conferred on me to-day.

The Chairman then called upon the Hon. OLIVER AMES, Lieutenant-Governor of Massachusetts, who spoke as follows : —

Mr. PRESIDENT, — On a spring morning, about thirty-five years ago, my grandfather said to me : " I wish you to take the express-wagon and drive to Dorchester to get a lot of pear-trees." He also said that his trees did not grow such pears as he found in Boston ; that he wanted the best, and the place to get the best was at Marshall P. Wilder's. I started on my journey with a letter of instructions, and when I reached Dorchester I presented it to Colonel Wilder. This was the first time I ever met our honored guest. Although I was a mere boy, he showed me great attention and kindness. He was then, as now and always, the same courteous, affable, and considerate gentleman. I got the pear-trees, and they have proved, all these years, the soundness of my grandfather's assertion, that Marshall P. Wilder's pear-trees were the best. From that day to this, I have always had the greatest respect for our honored guest, and I know that both my father and my grandfather held him in the highest esteem. In fact, it was almost an article in our family creed, to honor, respect, and revere Marshall P. Wilder.

The Hon. JOHN E. RUSSELL, Secretary of the State Board of Agriculture, was called upon to respond for that institution, and spoke as follows : —

Mr. PRESIDENT, and GENTLEMEN, — An occasion like this cannot be complete without reference to the active part taken by Mr. Wilder in the establishment of the State Board of Agriculture.

Like the comprehensive scheme for agricultural education that resulted in the State College, the plan of the State Board was formed at the instance of Mr. Wilder. It was voted at a meeting of the Trustees of the Norfolk Society, held Jan. 28, 1851, " That the President and Secretary be a Committee to mature and adopt a plan for a convention of delegates from the various Agricultural Societies of the Commonwealth, to be holden at some convenient time and place; the object of which shall be to concert measures for their mutual advantage, and for the promotion of the cause of Agricultural Education."

In accordance with this vote a convention of delegates was held at the State House on the 20th of March, 1851, of which Mr. Wilder was made president; among the vice-presidents was the venerable Ex-Governor Lincoln, of Worcester. This important convention became a permanent body, under the name of the Central Board of Agriculture.

In the following year this Board addressed a petition to the Legislature, asking for the formation of a Department of Agriculture, with offices commensurate with the importance of the duties to be discharged. This petition led to the establishment of the present Board of Agriculture.

It was fortunate for the new Board that it found at the outset a young, earnest, and competent secretary in the Hon. Charles L. Flint, now here by my side, who performed his important duties with a zeal and fidelity that made our Board respected in every part of the civilized world. Laws promoting our interests were proposed and carried through the Legislature, farmers' clubs were encouraged, important experiments were undertaken, and pleuro-pneumonia was extirpated from our herds.

From the beginning, the Board has had the advantage of Mr. Wilder's earnest leadership, wide agricultural knowledge, and sound judgment. Neither age, inclemency of weather, nor pressing occupations have kept him from participation in its meetings. To him the agriculture of the Commonwealth owes a debt that can never be paid; the records of our Board are a monument of his good works more enduring than brass. And, Sir, in view of his venerable years, so lightly borne, his interest in all

the active affairs of men, and his continued powers
of social enjoyment, I may well repeat the wish of
the poet Horace, expressed in one of his invoca-
tions to the Emperor Augustus, — *Serus in cœlum
redeas.*

The Boston Club, consisting of about twenty members, entered the dining-hall, and, through their President, JOHN L. STEVENSON, Esq., presented the congratulations of the Club to Colonel Wilder in the following words : —

The members of the Boston Club, dining in an adjacent room, could not permit this rare occasion to pass without calling in a body to testify by their presence their appreciation of the noble qualities of head and heart, which have so long added lustre to your honored name.

Accept, dear Sir, our sincere congratulations that at the age of fourscore years and five, in good health and vigor, you sit at this festal board, surrounded by honored and honoring friends, who have gathered here to felicitate you on this your natal day.

And that your silvered head may gladden our sight, while the golden love of your heart finds expression in the eloquent words of your lips on many happy returns of this delightful occasion, is our heartfelt wish.

Colonel WILDER responded as follows : —

GENTLEMEN, — You take me by surprise; but I assure you that I am most grateful for this mark of respect and desire for my future happiness. Your

Association is engaged in the worthy object of promoting the commerce, industry, and wealth of our city. Your fealty to the cause is aptly shown by your weekly patronage of the Parker-House larder, whereby you most faithfully exhibit not only your loyalty and enterprise in the promotion of these interests, but your capacity and ability to consume and carry off in sobriety the good things set before you.

The Club retired, each of them taking the hand of Colonel Wilder as they left the room.

His Honor, ALBERT PALMER, Mayor of the city of Boston, was called upon, and responded as follows : —

Mr. PRESIDENT, and GENTLEMEN, — Great deeds and memorable events have always been considered worthy of celebration. Their commemoration by public fête and festival marks the virtue of the race and promotes it. But a great and good life is the greatest deed and the best event that ever finds a record on this planet. The earth itself has no reason for existence except to perfect the race and produce the noblest types of manhood. We do a fitting thing, then, to honor a noble life approaching its completion ; to gaze with love and reverence upon the full-orbed sun before it touches the western horizon.

Gentlemen, the life of Marshall P. Wilder has fulfilled every demand of success and honor. On many and various fields of high endeavor he has demonstrated the power and virtue of a great man. In private business he has made fortunes honorably and honestly, and he has generously and wisely used them in works and plans of public beneficence and private charity. A merchant of highest repute and largest enterprise, he has a yet broader and more enviable fame among the farmers of New England,

for he has done more to promote and dignify their
occupation than any other man in America. In
horticulture, the *belles-lettres* of farming, he has
wrought miracles, and made it possible for every
home to have its Eden. He has shown that man
may still walk with God in the garden in the cool of
the day. Time would fail me to recount his great
and honorable services to society and the State. It
must suffice to say that no name of this century
is written more imperishably in the affection and
esteem of Boston and Massachusetts than the name
of him, our honored guest, whose birthday we greet
and bless to-night. With upright form, with clear
vision and unclouded intellect, he still stands before
us and walks among us, as wise as ever, as eloquent
as ever, and so good that there is no need of his
ever growing better; and our prayer is that he may
return late to the heavens, but that when he must
ascend, his mantle may fall upon us.

Professor J. C. Greenough, President of the Massachusetts Agricultural College, was called upon, and spoke as follows : —

Mr. President, and Gentlemen, — It is a pleasure to be here to-day, and to be permitted, as representative of the State College, to render a brief tribute to the value of the public services of our honored friend. To say that the Massachusetts Agricultural College owes its existence to him, would be but a very inadequate statement of what Colonel Wilder has done for the Commonwealth and for our whole country.

The power and the value of his efforts are best estimated by considering the change wrought in public opinion. Most of us remember that in our boyhood the opinion was almost universal, that a farmer needed little, if any, education beyond the ability to read, to write, and to perform the simpler operations in numbers. The value to the artisan of scientific knowledge and intellectual culture was not appreciated.

Though involved in the toil and the care inseparable from his mercantile career, Colonel Wilder, in the might of his manhood, with all his culture, his enthusiasm, and his force of character, gave himself to the great work of helping those who co-operate

with Nature in the ministries of the garden and the
field.

It has so passed into history, that no one of us
to-day need fail to present to himself that memorable
occasion in 1849, when Colonel Wilder addressed
the Norfolk Agricultural Society upon the value
of education to those engaged in productive industries, and urged the establishment of an agricultural
school or college.

In that audience were gathered the representative
men of New England. The address secured the profound attention and won the cordial approval of Levi
Lincoln, Josiah Quincy, president of Harvard University, Horace Mann, Charles Francis Adams, Robert
C. Winthrop, Edward Everett, Daniel Webster, and
others whom history will join with these. Nor did
the eloquent arguments of that address rest with the
auditors; thousands of copies were published, and
found their way to the firesides of thoughtful readers
in every part of our land.

The intense efforts which followed, when, as leader
in the Senate of Massachusetts, Colonel Wilder secured the passage of a bill providing for the establishment of an agricultural school or college, only
to meet with defeat in the House; his undaunted
energy in organizing for ultimate victory in the
midst of defeat; the many and varied forms of his
efforts until the college was established: all this

we would, if time permitted, gladly recount, not only
to render just meed of praise to him in whose honor
we have assembled, but to reinforce our own wearied
virtue in our toils for the public good.   With in-
creasing years, Colonel Wilder's zeal for the college
has never waned.   He has ever been a leading member of the Board of Trustees; he has transferred
from his own grounds to those of the college some
of his choicest plants; he has gracefully preserved
the early history of the college in his address, delivered on the occasion of the graduation of the first
class ; and in many other ways he has so cared for
the interests of the college, that he is justly regarded
as its founder and peerless supporter.

The line of buildings which to-day, at Amherst
graces one of the fairest landscapes in New England,
and the sound and practical education which they
were built to secure, are to be a lasting monument to his foresight, his patriotism, and his eloquent
persuasion.

The Hon. ALEXANDER H. RICE, Ex-Governor of Massachusetts, spoke in behalf of the merchants of Boston : —

Mr. PRESIDENT, and GENTLEMEN, — I esteem it a great privilege, as well as a great pleasure, to come here this evening and participate in these well-earned honors to our venerable and esteemed fellow-citizen. He stands alone in years and in vigorous activity united; and thus the tribute to him must be distinctive, personal, and emphatic. In the address from him to which we have just listened, so full of wonderful reminiscence, so full of moving pathos, he has told us that he is the oldest living merchant, bank director, and underwriter now in active service in Boston; that he looks back to the days when the trade of the city, though large for the time, was but the beginning of the vast bulk represented in the mercantile transactions of modern times. He has told us, too, that his participation in affairs antedates the building of steamboats, railroads, and other rapid means of communication, and runs back to the simplicity of a period immediately succeeding the colonial days, and before the forces of Nature had been so largely harnessed into the service of men.

That was an interesting year in which to have been born, whose eighty-fifth anniversary we are now cele-

brating. Washington and many of his contempora-
ries were still alive, and all the social and political elevation which his great services and illustrious example
had inspired were resplendent in their noonday glory.
Franklin, the great mechanic and practical philosopher, had lately died, and the maxims of prudence
which he had supplemented with a flood of wisdom
in all branches of public economy were diffusing
their influence throughout the country. Not only
was there no steamboat and no railroad, as our honored guest has said, but the steam-engine was but
little known, and Franklin and the scientists had
gone no further with electricity than to show that
it and lightning were the same. Boston was even
then a well-known commercial town, the most famous
on this continent. As the phrase goes, " her commerce whitened every sea " in reality; and the long
voyages beyond the Capes, to the Indian Ocean
and to farther parts of the East, as well as to all
latitudes of the Pacific coast, were so exclusively
hers, that to the native traders in their localities
the names " American " and " Bostonian," were
synonymous. The enterprise and intelligence of
her business men, and their accumulated wealth
and the liberality with which it was dispensed and
enjoyed, gave them the distinctive title of " merchant
princes": the only smack of royalty which they
would have tolerated even by implication.

Such was the generation of Boston merchants under whose tutelage Mr. Wilder came, in the commencement of his business career; and during the whole of it he has not only sustained the honorable renown which they had earned and have transmitted, but he has so kept pace with every new fact in knowledge, and so applied what he has gained in other pursuits than that of trade, as greatly to beautify life to others, and to secure for himself a distinction which is at once unique and conspicuous. Agriculture brings the products of her bountiful harvests as a testimony of his services to her; Horticulture, her beautiful trophies to be woven into a garland for his birthday anniversary; and Pomology, her luscious fruits as fit symbols of a life ripening into its maturity, yet preserving its flavor and richness. There is hardly a public enterprise of the last three generations, scarcely a pursuit in life, or an institution of patriotism, discipline, or charity, that does not bear the signet of his touch and feel the vigor of his co-operation. Why, Sir, it may be said, almost with literal truth, that the trees which this great arborist has planted and cultivated and loved are not more numerous than the evidences of his handiwork in all the useful and beneficent departments of life; and all the flowers that shall grow to the end of time ought to bear fragrance to his memory.

General JOSHUA L. CHAMBERLAIN, Ex-Governor of Maine, and late President of Bowdoin College, was called upon, and responded as follows : —

Mr. PRESIDENT, — I should be sorry, indeed, if words were such bad servants as to desert me when the call is to express the pleasure I feel at being so opportunely in this house as to be invited to join you in paying this tribute of respect to a citizen whose good deeds are so various, so extensive, and so long continued, and whose character is as widely honored as it is well-known.

The name of an "old Boston merchant" is a title of honor the world over. The preserver of historic character and fame who transmits the high virtues of our ancestors to the present and future generations, renders a service for which his country owes him thanks. It happens, however, that within the circles most familiar to my younger days, the name of our venerated guest is associated with another service which it is not too much to say is more widely felt and scarcely less widely known and honored than either of the others. His is a household name where choice fruits and flowers gladden the gardens and the home-circle.

This work of our friend is a high art. Merely to imitate Nature is but an humble form of art. But

to improve upon Nature; to tame her wild, harsh
tones; to prune her wayward ruggedness and barren
shoots; to guard against natural enemies; to banish
the germs of disease and death; to cherish best possibilities; to regenerate, beautify, and perfect her:
this is a true art, and a token of man's superior
nature. It is a beautiful privilege to enter thus into
communion with Nature, to stand at the source and
fountain of her gifts, to see her mysterious ways, to
learn her laws, to lay a sympathizing hand upon her
forces, and to win them to one's thought and guide
them at one's will. It is a noble art to direct these
powers to their own perfection and to human good.
The painter or the sculptor produces but the likeness
of things: a likeness, perhaps, which genius has
idealized and perfected, but only an image after all.
But here is an art which is true creation, which produces a real thing and a living thing. These things
are a science and an education: and so our honored
friend has made himself Master of Nature's arts, and
Doctor of her laws!

And as in every true art, what is for beauty is also
for service. It seems to be intended by the Author
of Nature that she should in all the fruits most sub-
servient to the life of man present but rude types,
yet susceptible of various perfectionments; and that
it is a necessary part of human development and
culture to bring out the possibilities of her primitive

types. Neglected, they return to their crude form, and become a bane and not a blessing. The command to subdue the earth was a command to cultivate it; and this was for man's sake as well as for Nature's. We are told, on highest authority, that ages ago the earth was cursed for man's sin; and some have been cynical enough to say that our New-England soil, and to a somewhat extreme degree our good State of Massachusetts, had got more than her fair share of it: of the curse, I mean, not the sin! But I half remember, Dr. Blagden will prompt me if I cannot get through, that that shrewd old Hebrew speech had a word which meant either to bless or to curse, according as you took things. There was a deep philosophy in that. Curses are blessings taken wrong end foremost! Blessings are curses if you do not take them by the right handles! The good if dishonored, becomes an evil and a destroyer. So it may not be wholly wrong to fancy that the earth cursed for man's sin, was cursed also for his sake. If he fell by eating of the tree of knowledge of good and evil, then he must use that knowledge in working his way back by separating the good from the evil thus laid on Nature. If by eating an apple he fell from an angel's estate, he must learn to bring out an apple that will make a man an angel! Has not our friend done that? Has he not learned how to redeem the earth from its curse? It is glory enough for a man to leave the world better than he found it.

There is another thing. Such work gives strength. It is a good thing to take the touch of earth. There was deep significance in the old fable of Antæus, who in the wrestle against all comers took on new life whenever he touched the earth, and his final adversary only prevailed by lifting him into the air. But nobody ever got our friend into the air! When wearied with the various strifes of chance and fate, he turned to the earth and sprung up with new vigor every time. Such work reacts on character. A growth in grace, so to speak, runs along parallel with this development of nature. While one is thus working amidst the laws of life, and bringing out the thousand utilities that lie hidden in the earth, it is but a natural analogy that he should bring out also those expressions of infinite beauty and service that lie in the possibilities of the human soul. Who can look on this expressive countenance, and not feel that he has found this grace, and realized this exceeding great reward? We rejoice in this honored old age, this youth, rounded, beautified, and sweetened into supreme manhood; and we rejoice also that it shall remain for after times an example and inspiration for all who would live true lives, and win the honor that comes here and hereafter to noble character.

The Hon. FREDERICK SMYTH, Ex-Governor of New Hampshire, Vice-President of the United States Agricultural Society, spoke as follows : —

Mr. PRESIDENT, and GENTLEMEN, — I count it a high honor and great privilege to sit at this table with so many venerable and distinguished men of Massachusetts and New England; and especially so, on such an auspicious occasion as the birthday of my honored and venerated friend. Although associated with him officially in the United States Agricultural Society, the American Pomological Society, and other organizations, for more than thirty years, I have been his pupil, sitting at his feet and learning what I could, not only of scientific pursuits akin to agriculture, but of those graces and virtues as well which adorn the civilization of our time; and, while revering him as a master, loving him as a friend above most other men whom it has been my good fortune to know.

The President of your Agricultural College has told us how much Colonel Wilder has done for the schools and colleges of Massachusetts. Why, Mr. President, I consider Marshall P. Wilder a college himself, a great university, from which has gone out to the people a knowledge made practical by the tests of his expe-

rience.   To minister to the delight of the eye, or to
the pleasure of a healthy and refined appetite, is an
object worthy of any man's attainment; and so thousands may bless the thoughtful care of that public
benefactor whose wealth, acquired in an honorable
mercantile career, has been devoted to such wonderful
improvements in the fruits and flowers of our land.

Mr. President, and Gentlemen, I have the honor to
represent here the State which claims with pride to
be the birthplace of our honored friend.   The people
of New Hampshire to-night greet Marshall P. Wilder
on the eighty-fifth anniversary of his birth, and they
hope and pray that his life may be spared yet many
years to bless those who have so many reasons to
bless him.   And I know they are proud to have
given so good and so great a man to Massachusetts.

New Hampshire once had a distinguished son
whom she delighted to honor as a great man at home,
but it was said that when he was called to spread
himself over the whole land he was rather thin; but
here is one who, if I may so speak, has spread himself not only over our States and Territories, but over
lands across the sea, a genial and gentle ruler, and
yet with no diminution of his substantial presence,
or in all that is glorious and lovable.   God still continue to bless Marshall P. Wilder, until glorified
above !

Ex-Governor NATHANIEL P. BANKS, U. S. Marshal, was called upon, and responded as follows : —

Mr. PRESIDENT, — It has given me great pleasure to participate in the well-deserved and generous honors paid to the distinguished citizen who is the guest of this occasion. I cannot say, as so many gentlemen have said, that I did not expect to be called upon for a speech. One might as well think to sit at a Parker-House banquet, celebrated the world over, and not partake of the feast, as to listen to the praises of a citizen whose whole life marks one of the golden periods of human existence, and not venture, after the well-nigh universal American custom, less honored by the observance than the breach, I think, either to enlarge the scope of approval or echo the praises sounded by others. And yet I confess I am ill prepared to do what I well know should be done upon an occasion of such personal and public interest.

It is rare good fortune that has vouchsafed to our honored guest the ripe and wholesome age of four-score and five years, passed in such peaceful and pleasant places, attended by such beneficent influences, such remarkable activity as are exhibited in his career. Shakspeare makes one of the greatest of his

characters say, in delineating the events closing a
long and tempestuous career, that "Age is unnecessary." In the sense that no person and no life
can be indispensable to a full development of the
majestic and inscrutable laws of Nature, we may well
say that age is not an essential element of the destiny of men and events. But such a sheaf of years
and honors, the fruits of uninterrupted and long-
continued meritorious service as gentlemen have re-
vealed to us, must be taken into any account current
of civilization, and welcomed as providential occur-
rences in the lives of men and nations. They illus-
trate the commencement as well as the close of his
life. Youth and age are alike distinguished and
honored in him. In every direction his path is lu-
minous. He has been a tireless student of Nature,
a bold investigator, audacious in experiment, fertile
in resources, prodigal of labor, unselfish and even
lavish in the distribution of the fruits of his study
and toil. It was thus at a time when our people
were incredulous and hopeless as to improvement
in the ordinary methods of industry and labor, and
especially in the cultivation of the soil and its in-
numerable products, that he opened to us affluent
and endless sources of local and national wealth.

But it interests me less to speculate on what he
has done (indeed, nothing is left unsaid in that
direction) than to inquire by what occult methods

or powers he has accomplished so much in so many
useful yet divergent walks of life. In speaking of
different religions which have been received and
cherished by men, Mr. Gibbon, the historian, says
that the Christians adopted the religion of the Jews,
adding to it one element: an element of supernal
power indeed: Sociability. What widespread and
beneficent changes has it not wrought in secular as
well as in religious affairs, by concert of action among
men of good will and good works! It elevated fami-
lies into races, villages into kingdoms, that in the
steady progress of their triumphs " sang *Te Deums* in
nations rather than in choirs." The growth of such
organizations continued through centuries, until age
appeared an indispensable and vital rather than a
superfluous ally, and permanent success was assured
in the perpetual union of beneficent institutions and
principles.

It is easy for us to see in what manner affability,
courtesy, personal integrity, confidence, courage, and
endurance, qualities which influence individuals as
sociability affects civilization, have contributed to
his success in the numerous and important social
and national enterprises which make the character
and career of our distinguished guest illustrious.
I can scarcely enumerate, much less analyze or
characterize them, and therefore limit myself to
special notice of but one: his connection with the

oldest military organization of the Republic of the United States, *The Ancient and Honorable Artillery Company.*

This ancient and well-styled " Honorable" company of citizen-soldiers was incorporated in 1638, eight years after the settlement of Boston, and has continued two hundred and forty-five years in uninterrupted and meritorious service. During Shays's Rebellion, the Governor and other officers of the State often met the Ancients at Faneuil Hall in consultation upon military affairs. The company has had many illustrious commanders. Mr. Wilder was the one hundred and fifty-fifth in regular succession, elected in 1856. The volunteer militia of Massachusetts was not then honored as it has been at later periods. In the discussion of the constitution, in 1853, it was urged (not by reformers or non-resistants only, but by eminent citizens of high rank in civil and military service), that the militia should be organized for police service only, and that no soldier in any case should be required to leave the State except upon his own consent, nor even then except to accompany the Governor. At public celebrations, on national anniversaries, the best organized military companies were assailed with burning words of scorn and derision. A few years later, fewer than could have been anticipated at that time, Massachusetts had ordered one hundred and fifty-three thousand of her troops to

invade insurgent States of the republic, and other
States and Territories increased the number to very
nearly three million defenders of the Union.

It is unnecessary to say that our guest gave his
own energy and spirit to the Ancient and Honorable
Artillery Company while he commanded it. This
corps has been honored in other States as a just type
of past military organizations. Much of its renown at
home and abroad is due to its one hundred and fifty-
fifth commander. Recognizing its connection with
the Ancient Royal Artillery of London, often commanded by the sovereigns of England, and at that
time by His Royal Highness Prince Albert, Prince
Consort, he opened with him a correspondence which
led to the enrolment of Prince Albert, and later of
the present Prince of Wales, as Special Honorary
Members of the Ancient and Honorable Artillery
of Boston. Both companies are recognized in English and American history as representing the best
type of military veterans.

It is fortunate that during this period the relations
of England and America were so administered by
the pre-eminent English and American statesmen of
that day, that no untoward word or deed disturbed
the profound peace that reigned between the two
countries. We are for that reason relieved from the
painful duty of speculating upon results that might
have changed the even balance of nations, if those

ancient corps had met in the dread shock of battle,
commanded by the PRINCE CONSORT and the PRINCE
MERCHANT!

Alexander wept, they say, when told in his youth
that no more worlds remained for him to conquer.
Our honored exemplar, guest, and friend, in a ripe
old age, with greater wisdom, smiles to see that for
him there are no more impossibilities over which he
can triumph. So numerous and so striking are his
trophies, that it seems even for us, emulators of his
fame, there are no more impossibilities to conquer!
But there is one left, for us, for our successors, for all
men : the impossibility of finding another MARSHALL
PINCKNEY WILDER!

The Hon. LEVERETT SALTONSTALL, Vice-President of the Massachusetts Society for the Promotion of Agriculture, responded for that Society as follows : —

Mr. PRESIDENT, and GENTLEMEN, — I accepted with great pleasure your very kind invitation to this dinner in honor of our venerable friend, the Hon. Marshall P. Wilder, who has completed his eighty-fifth year, and is with us to-day as fresh and vigorous in his appearance as he is in intellect; and though I had not thought, in the presence of so many distinguished guests, to be called upon to speak on this occasion, yet it gives me unqualified pleasure to add my congratulations to swell the chorus of affection and respect which arises from so many full hearts.

Sir, I doubt if there has ever been so exceptional a gathering as this in honor of one during his life, at so advanced an age; and I trust it may in some measure recompense Colonel Wilder for his many generous and useful services rendered not only to his friends and neighbors, but to the State and Nation. Eminent as a merchant, he is equally distinguished in the arts of horticulture and agriculture. He has bestowed years of careful thought and untiring zeal in inspiring a love for them among his fellow-men; and for the good his enthusiasm in these pursuits has accomplished, his name will long be held in deepest respect and gratitude.

He says he is proud of his success as a merchant, for it is as such that he has secured the means to carry into effect his generous designs in other directions. He well might add that he is grateful for his love of the field and the garden, for to them he owes that freshness of nature and vigor of mind which have brought success to him in business.

It was my privilege to be associated with him for several years in the State Board of Agriculture, where his interest in the work of the Board, and his watchfulness for its advancement, were most conspicuous. Truly, to him is "the hoary head a crown of glory." His life is a lesson to the young and the old, and I wish they would study his well-balanced character as their best example.   May he be long spared to us!

THE Hon. FRANCIS B. HAYES, President of the Massachusetts Horticultural Society, responded for that association as follows : —

Mr. PRESIDENT, and GENTLEMEN, — You have assigned to me the agreeable duty of speaking for the Massachusetts Horticultural Society on this interesting occasion, and especially in reference to the connection of our honored guest with it.

Let us recall the past, and briefly recount some of the incidents of his life.

In an inland village in New Hampshire, at the commencement of the present century, might be seen a little boy instructed at his mother's knee in the principles of morality and religion, which he has never forgotten. Soon after, we see him a diligent pupil in the district school. When old enough, he engages in rural pursuits, until he is induced, by the laudable desire of supporting himself and improving his condition, to engage in such business occupations as opportunity presents to him in his native place. Growing ambitious to take a more prominent position in life, he leaves his native town, with the respect of all the neighborhood, and enters upon a successful business career in this city; passing through all the grades of advancement by which the

worthy and industrious young man rises, till he is
an active member of one of the leading mercantile
houses of the country.

But the love of Nature possesses his soul, and,
while not neglecting his business duties, we find
him deeply interested in agricultural and horticultural subjects; and thus he is brought in contact
with older men of similar tastes. When a little
more than thirty years of age, we see him associated with Dearborn, Lowell, Story, Everett, and
others, engaged in the study and practice of the science and art of horticulture, and the founders and
supporters of the Massachusetts Horticultural Society.
All acknowledge his zeal and wisdom in forwarding
the objects of that Society. Soon he is placed at
its head, and diligently and faithfully guards and promotes its interests, as its President, for eight years.
During this period the Society attained a much more
elevated position than it had ever before reached. He
continues, after retiring from office, to be a leading
member of the Society, notwithstanding the cares of
business and the distractions of political life, which
his fellow-citizens insist upon his entering, occupy
his attention. A devoted lover of Nature, he will
not abandon this love, whatever may be the temp-
tations to do so. He is the President of the American Pomological Society, which office he has held
thirty-four years, and was President of the United

States Agricultural Society for several years; he is senior member of the State Board of Agriculture, and holds many other offices of trust and honor; yet he continues to remain one of the main stays of the Massachusetts Horticultural Society, a constant attendant at its meetings, and an earnest and active guardian of its concerns. I stand now in the presence of many members of that Society, and I remember the important and valuable services of Dearborn and Lowell, of Bigelow, Hunnewell, the Hoveys, the Brecks, the Mannings, Whitmore, Strong, Hyde, Parkman, Gray, and many others; yet I think the members of the Society will unanimously concur with me in the opinion that no one has been a more prominent friend of this institution, no one has done more, if so much, for the cause of horticulture in this community, by his tongue, his pen, and his various labors, as the honored guest of this evening.

Mr. Chairman, I cannot but allude to the benevolence and kindness of heart of our venerable friend, and the religious element which is at the foundation of his character. Notwithstanding the eminent positions he has occupied, notwithstanding the high esteem and respect his life has commanded, and though social elevation is not infrequently attended with hauteur and reserve, separating apparently the more distinguished from those less highly favored, yet our friend always shows himself the simple Chris-

tian gentlemen, easily accessible, and ready to serve
all to the extent of his ability. His life and character
recall to me the beautiful lines of Sir Henry Wotton,
when he describes the good and truly happy man : —

> " Who God doth late and early pray
> More of his grace than gifts to lend ;
> And entertains the harmless day
> With a religious book or friend."

Long, long may the life of our venerable friend be
spared to us ! for in him the community has a most
worthy citizen, the associations with which he is connected a wise counsellor and safe guide, and all of us
a true friend.

The Hon. DANIEL NEEDHAM, Secretary of the New England Agricultural Society, spoke in behalf of that Society as follows : —

Mr. PRESIDENT, and GENTLEMEN, — It gives me great pleasure to be present on this occasion, and give utterance to a word of testimony commemorative of the eighty-fifth anniversary of the distinguished guest who sits at your right hand. I have long had the honor of the acquaintance of Marshall P. Wilder; and as I have studied his labors of usefulness and beneficence, I have grown into an admiration of the man, which has been shared, as I well know, not only by a few friends, but by communities of men limited by no geographical lines. The name of Marshall P. Wilder is historic; his labors in Agriculture and Horticulture, two great industries which underlie the prosperity of States and Nations, have made his name immortal, and indelibly inscribed it upon the scroll of great and distinguished men in all nationalities. Well may we, as his neighbors and friends, come together to give emphasis to our admiration; and well might we, as citizens of a great nation, even were he not our personal friend, come together to emphasize the honor which his name and his labors have conferred upon our country and the world. Sir, his name is as imperishable as the granite hills among which he was born.

4

The Rev. EDWARD N. PACKARD, Minister of the Second Church, Dorchester, was called upon, and responded as follows : —

Mr. PRESIDENT, — I owe my invitation, on this occasion, to the fact that I stand in the relation of pastor to our venerable guest. I count it a great honor to be in such a succession of ministers as the Second Church in Dorchester shows. Colonel Wilder was for many years the intimate friend of the first pastor of that church, the Rev. Dr. Codman. He joined in welcoming the Rev. Dr. Means, as next in succession, and proved himself for thirty years, while Dr. Means held the office, a most valued friend and helper to his minister. It was a great pleasure to me, when a few years ago I returned to New England, to be so cordially welcomed and heartily supported by this beloved parishioner, whose name stands on the call which I received, and who for more than fifty years has been a most conspicuous figure in the parish. " Without all contradiction, the less is blessed of the better."

The relation of a pastor to his people is unlike any other. No ties of friendship are more intimate or more sacred. How much the minister depends upon the affection, the counsel, and the encouragement which the faithful and considerate parishioner may bring to him!

Mr. President, I represent here to-night, very imperfectly it is true, that Power which claims at least one seventh of a man's living hours. There comes a day in each week when, by common consent, there is a truce in the great world's warfare and toil. There comes a day, Gentlemen, when all the strain and struggle of your commerce, all the pursuits of your agriculture, cease, and man can turn his thoughts to higher things. And it is these higher things that give value to the lower; it is the carrying of the higher into the lower that redeems them and makes them blessings. Everything, indeed, rests in something higher than itself: the material in the spiritual. What we see here to-night, these fruits and flowers developed by human taste and skill: this is the higher and the spiritual invading the material and using it for its own ends. I believe that the coming of the kingdom of heaven will be by the interpenetration of the earthly by the heavenly. I believe that the time will come when, literally, it shall be true that "the wilderness and the solitary place shall be glad because of Him, and the desert shall rejoice and blossom as the rose."

I am glad to be here, Mr. President, and join with you in this heart-felt tribute of affection and veneration to Colonel Wilder. Do we not all hope that when the time comes for him to draw near the other world, the gates of the heavenly paradise may open before him, and no sword of cherubim may bar his entrance?

The Rev. EDMUND F. SLAFTER, Corresponding Secretary of the New England Historic Genealogical Society, was called upon, and spoke as follows : —

Mr. PRESIDENT, and GENTLEMEN, — The occasion which has brought us together naturally turns our thoughts to the little rural town of Rindge, on the southern borders of New Hampshire, in whose history one of the most interesting features is the birth of a boy-baby, which occurred eighty-five years ago to-day. The parents were so young that in *law* they and their young scion were *infants* together. The father had not attained his majority, and the mother was still younger. If, in general, we regard it an act of imprudence to organize a family at so early an age, nevertheless, in this particular case, I am sure, we shall all be agreed that the enterprising young couple could not have done a wiser or a better thing. I was told to-day, by a lady, that every mother expects, when she gives birth to a son, that he will some day be President of the United States. What forecastings that young mother, on the borders of New Hampshire, had, as she gazed upon her baby-boy while he lay slumbering in the new cradle that had just been brought into the house, or in the old one that had come down as an heirloom in the family, I know not; but if her prescience pictured to her mind what he was really and actually to become, she must have felt a truer and loftier pride than she could have experienced in the belief that he would attain, by the crooked ways now too often practised, to the chief magistracy of this great nation.

Sixteen years ago I was appointed, by the New England Historic Genealogical Society, chairman of a committee to nominate a president for that association, a vacancy having just occurred by the death of the lamented Governor Andrew. It was important that the occupant of the chair of that great Society, then numbering not less than eight hundred members (men of high standing and character in all the New England States, and indeed in other States of the Union and in other countries), should possess eminent and peculiar qualifications. In looking through our large membership, our attention was soon directed to the Hon. Marshall P. Wilder. We traced his career from his boyhood onward, in the school, the academy; his brief apprenticeship on his father's farm and in his father's store; in the establishment of a business for himself; his removal to the metropolis; his prudent beginning, and steady progress for many years, always advancing, never receding; and then, after the lapse of forty years, still a Boston merchant in one of the largest and most respected mercantile houses in the city: in all this we found an element of character which we desired in the future President of our Society.

Our attention was also attracted by his military career, not in war, but in peace. Happily, no war occurred during the strength of his manhood to call him into the public service. In his native State he was enrolled in the militia at sixteen, was quarter-master-sergeant at eighteen, adjutant of a regiment at twenty-one, captain of a company at twenty-two, lieutenant-colonel at twenty-four, and colonel of a regiment at twenty-six years of age: thus early ob-taining the military title which is so familiar to us in connection with his name, and which he has now borne through a period of more than sixty years. In Boston he was commander of the Ancient and Honorable Artillery Company, chartered in 1638, the oldest military organization in the United States. His splendid physique, his natural dignity, and his graceful bearing were in fine accord with all these positions, which he successively filled, and to which, by his presence and influence, he gave a new value and importance. His military tastes and services were to us, Mr. President, no objection in the man whom we desired as President of our Society.

But again we found that the proclivity of his mind, as clearly evinced in his boyhood when he tried his hand at the plough and the hoe on his father's farm,

sprang from a root far down in the deep recesses
of his nature, and could not be repressed or extin-
guished by other occupations and pursuits. At an
early period, first as a recreation, and afterward with
a higher purpose, he became a gentleman farmer in
name, but really a practical and scientific farmer
in its truest and noblest meaning. The relation of
soils to specific products was studied and made the
subject of experiment; and this not for himself
alone, but for the great farming public of the nation.
Fruit-trees and fruit-culture, flora-culture and flora-
hybridizing, and a proper nomenclature in pomology,
received his careful and assiduous attention; and
these labors have been followed by the most satis-
factory results. He has always been a profound
believer in organized and associated effort, and his
name has been connected from the start with those
great associations in this line which have so marvel-
lously elevated and dignified agricultural pursuits.
He was the organizer and first President of the Norfolk Agricultural Society, which office he held for
twenty years; the first President of the Central Board,
the forerunner and parent of our State Board of
Agriculture; the organizer, and the first President,
of the United States Agricultural Society at Washington; the organizer, likewise, of the American
Pomological Society in New York, in 1848, of which
he was the first President (and I may add that he

has been President of that Society, with the excep-
tion of one term, down to the present moment); he
was at the front in the establishment of our Agricultural College, was the first trustee elected on its
Board, and was present and delivered a discourse
to its first class at their graduation.   The Massachusetts Institute of Technology is also indebted to
him from its start for valuable service.   His interest
in these institutions has never faltered, his hand has
never been weary, his voice never silent, and his pen
never idle.   His addresses on agriculture, embracing
horticulture and pomology, and on other subjects, are
exceedingly numerous, and are full of valuable infor-
mation, clothed in language at once clear, vivacious,
and inspiring.

We found, also, in this survey, that Colonel Wilder
had been a member of both houses of the Legislature of the State, and of the Governor's Council, and
President of the Massachusetts Senate.   In all these
public positions in which he had been placed by the
suffrage of his scrutinizing fellow-citizens, in all these
public acts and doings, we found that he was many-
sided, that his nature was broad and expansive, that
he had a great heart and a clear head, realizing in
himself the old Latin maxim, *Humani nihil alienum;*
that nothing was unworthy of his consideration which
relates to the welfare of man.   I need hardly inform
you, Mr. President, and Gentlemen, that when we pre-

sented his name as President of our Society, his election was carried by a unanimous vote; and now for
sixteen years he has been annually re-elected without
a dissenting voice; and for the last few years, as a
mark of special respect and reverence, the members
have risen in their seats to receive the announcement
of his election.

I have thus touched upon some of the reasons, Mr.
President, and Gentlemen, which influenced the action of the Society which I have here the honor to
represent.   When Colonel Wilder became President,
in 1868, the Society had been established twenty-
three years; it had a large membership, a library of
eight thousand volumes, which had floated in from
members and others almost entirely as gifts, with
some valuable manuscripts, and a thousand dollars in
funds.   This constituted the whole property of the
Society.   It was certainly a good beginning for a
historical association, starting out on a new line of
investigation.   But a great Society, having a great
purpose, could not bestow its library conveniently for
use, or increase it to meet the growing demands,
in a rented flat of uncertain tenure in a mercantile
building.

Soon after Colonel Wilder became President of
the Society, a building committee was appointed,
of which he was chairman, whose business it was to
erect or purchase a suitable building, and perform the

uninviting task of obtaining the money to pay for it.
However difficult it may be for us to believe that
it was an easy task to accomplish this work, nevertheless, within a few months after the undertaking
was begun, the sum of forty-two thousand dollars
was secured for the purpose, nearly all of which
was obtained by the personal solicitation of Colonel
Wilder himself; a house was purchased, remodelled,
and paid for, and is now the unencumbered property
of the Society. In addition to this he solicited, personally, with the assistance of one or two others, twelve
thousand dollars towards the endowment of the Society; and in his annual addresses he has called upon
members not to forget the Society in their testamen-
tary bequests. In response, several legacies have been
received, so that our funds to-day are more than forty-
two thousand dollars; to which, adding the cost of the
house, the amount is over eighty-four thousand dollars,
which has been added to our property since our honored guest was placed at the head of the institution.
Every other department has advanced in complete har-
mony with this. Our library has gone up from eight
thousand to more than eighteen thousand volumes; it
has more than doubled in numbers, and quadrupled
in working value. Our membership was then eight
hundred, and is now more than eleven hundred. Our
publications are more numerous, and richer in material. Our building has become crowded, and too

narrow for our needs; and our venerable and enterprising President has already obtained some important pledges for its proper enlargement.

In Colonel Wilder's relation to all this growth, I do
not mean to say that he has not had able, earnest,
efficient, and responsive co-workers. But I do mean
to say, that, by his annual addresses and appeals,
unfolding in numberless ways his appreciation of the
great value and importance of family and local history, and by his assiduous and unremitting labors,
and especially by the potency of his magnetic power
over the minds of other men, he has done much to
inspire not only the members of the Society, but the
great body of our New England population, with a
just love and interest in this line of study, and they
have consequently been ready and happy to furnish
the means and facilities for carrying on these important investigations.

I began, Mr. President, and Gentlemen, by pointing
out some of the reasons which induced us to ask our
distinguished guest to accept the Presidency of the
New England Historic Genealogical Society; and
now I venture to predict that he will continue to be
the President of that institution by the unanimous
suffrage of its members, so long as Providence
lengthens out his days, and so long as he is willing
to hold the important trust.

Major BEN: PERLEY POORE, Past Commander of the Ancient and Honorable Artillery Company, and Secretary of the United States Agricultural Society, was called upon, and spoke as follows : —

Mr. PRESIDENT, — It has been asserted that no general is a hero in the eyes of his orderly sergeant; but I, who have served in a subordinate capacity under Colonel Wilder, in the United States Agricultural Society and in the Ancient and Honorable Artillery Company, regard him as a hero. He has attained that distinction without having made a widow or an orphan, without having caused the loss of a drop of blood or a precious life; he has been the friend of religion and of education; he is a worthy and well-qualified brother of the mystic tie; he has actively sustained our parent military organization; he has secured the preservation of our historical and genealogical archives; he has improved our trees, plants, fruits, and flowers; and he has "caused two blades of grass to grow where but one grew before." What a noble record!

It has been my lot, Sir, as many at these tables know, to pass nearly six months of each of the last fifty years away from my ancestral acres in Massachusetts, and to have occupied a position in connection with

the press, that has enabled me to be somewhat behind the political curtain at Washington, and to know
what work each public servant there has performed.
When I first visited the National Capital some of the
old worthies were living, and the intellectual giants of
our nation were in their prime.   Webster, and Clay,
and Jackson, and Calhoun, and Benton, and Woodbury, with others of national renown, ruled the Republic with noble patriotism, and profound statesmanship,
and stern political virtue.   Since then the average
congressman, devoting himself to personal enrich-
ment, partisan scheming, and the mercenary lust for
office, has grown "small by degrees and beautifully
less;" while honorable citizens retire in disgust from
the rude jostlings of contending parties, unwilling to
act with those whom they cannot respect, and feeling
that "the post of honor is the private station."   It
has often occurred to me, how few of the scores and
hundreds of congressmen that I have known ever
originated, much less carried through, any measure
calculated to benefit his fellow-creatures.

How different, Sir, has been the career of our
parental friend, whose name is a household word in
every American heart, and whom we have met to-
night to honor!   He has always been distinguished
for his sound, useful common-sense, which has enabled him to be of great service to his friends.   The
man with every sense but common-sense is as help-

less as a child, when exposed to the rub and bustle of
the world; it is the philosopher over again, who,
when the vessel in which he was embarked was about
to founder at sea, having read much in books of
anchors of hope and anchors of safety, but knowing
nothing practically of their use, lashed himself to the
best bower, and then smiled in lofty pity at the igno-
rance of the poor creatures who were going to trust
themselves to rafts and planks. Colonel Wilder has
been prompted by good sense in organizing good
works; and with rare executive ability he has congre-
gated large masses of men, and raised large sums of
money, for the support of some great pursuit. He
has been a pioneer, or, more properly speaking, a
recruiting sergeant, for many invincible armies. As
it is inscribed on the dome of St. Paul's Cathedral,
in memory of its architect, *Lector, si monumentum
requiris, circumspice:* "If you seek his monument,
look around;" so we see Colonel Wilder's monument
around us here: men whom he recruited, and who
have, under his discipline, become centurions in the
hosts of religion, freemasonry, agriculture, horticulture, history, the arts, and the Ancient and Honorable
Artillery Company.

Ah! Mr. President, I can almost see some of the
old Past Commanders of that honored corps march
into this room with their bright steel breastplates,
their thick coats of buff-leather, and their helmets

crowned with scarlet plumes, to congratulate their successor, Colonel Wilder. Following them, would come those who fought gallantly in the Revolutionary war, in blue and buff, with their cocked hats and their shirt-ruffles. Next we should see those who distinguished themselves in the supplementary war with Great Britain in 1812, followed by those who served in the swamps of Florida, and those who bore the stars and stripes in triumph through the land of the Montezumas. Then would come those brave men, some of whom served under Colonel Wilder in time of peace, who were engaged in the war for the suppression of the Rebellion, from which the Union armies came marching home triumphantly, without a single star missing from their colors or from the national escutcheon. When General Augureau, of France, was asked what was wanting to add to the splendor of the scene at the coronation of the First Napoleon, he replied, "Nothing but the presence of our dead heroes, who died to perpetuate the Government!" Would that we could be honored to-night with the presence of those who preceded or served with Colonel Wilder in the Ancient and Honorable Artillery Company, but who now sleep in the soldier's grave, where they will remain until the last trumpet shall sound their reveille! Colonel Wilder is, Mr. President, the oldest living Past Commander of our old corps, and a glorious representative of his predecessors two hundred years ago: men famed in Church and State, who feared God and kept their powder dry.

The Ancient and Honorable Artillery Company, with its two hundred and forty-five years of service, greets its oldest Past Commander with love to-night, and presents arms! Its members present, with pleasing emotions knocking hard at the doors of their hearts, wish many more years of happiness to Colonel Wilder. Appreciating his honesty, his truth, his temperance, his courage, his patience, his forbearance, and the other bright virtues which shine in his character, our hopes are ever clustered around him, and our good wishes will ever attend him. Indeed, we are tempted to say to him to-night, in the language of the old Latins, *Esto perpetua :* " Be thou eternal ! "

Mr. President, I am confident that the distinguished gentlemen around these tables will long remember to-night, and recall with pleasure its varied homages to Colonel Wilder, thankful that we have so pure a shrine, so bright an oracle, as the common property of all who reverence virtue, admire manhood, or aspire to noble deeds. Succeeding years will not dim the freshness of Colonel Wilder's fame ; and the more frequently we drink at this fountain, the sweeter we shall find its waters.

> " You may break, you may shatter the vase, if you will,
> But the scent of the roses will hang round it still."

5

General FRANCIS A. WALKER, the President of the
Massachusetts Institute of Technology, responded as follows : —

Mr. PRESIDENT, — A biography of Colonel Wilder
would necessarily become, in a great measure, the
history of a score of institutions whose foundations
have been laid by his hands, or with his personal
co-operation.   Even those brief references to his life
and his life's work which are appropriate to an occasion like this, cannot fail to array before our minds
many of the most active and influential societies of
Boston, of Massachusetts, of New England, and of
the United States.

It must be interesting to every observer, it must
be deeply gratifying to our revered friend, to see
the representatives of such great and various and
beneficent institutions crowding this board to offer
their tributes of gratitude, respect, and affection to
the sage, philanthropist, and patriot, whose eighty-
fifth birthday is to-day celebrated amid the hearty
good wishes of thousands for his long continuance
in life, health, and happiness.

I trust that not the least useful to the community,
not the least honorable to our friend, among the
many institutions at whose foundation he has pre-

sided, and to whose enlargement he has contributed by wise counsel and generous assistance, is that on whose behalf I am called to respond : the Massachusetts Institute of Technology.

Colonel Wilder was one of the earliest and most earnest advocates of the views and measures which finally led to the establishment of this school of industrial science. As early as 1857, before the Back-Bay lands had been filled up, he became the chairman of a committee of citizens called together for the purpose of establishing a Conservatory of Arts and Sciences on those lands ; and when, later, that idea had taken more definite shape, he acted as chairman of the committee which drew up a memorial to the Legislature, urging the adoption of that scheme by the State of Massachusetts. In the following year, the same committee, under the same earnest and public-spirited chairman, presented another memorial to the Legislature. This effort was crowned with success, resulting in the charter of the Institute of Technology.

In the act of incorporation, which passed April 10, 1861, Colonel Wilder was named as a member of the Board of Trust. He became one of the vice-presidents of the new organization, and continued to act in that capacity until the office was abolished in the reorganization which took place some years ago under an amended charter.

Through all the early efforts to attract the attention of the Legislature and the people to the importance of industrial and art education, and through the severe struggles which so painfully tried the courage and the faith even of those who most strongly and ardently believed in the mission of the Institute, as well as through the happier years of fruition, while the efforts put forth in the days of darkness and despondency were bearing their harvest of success and fame, Colonel Wilder was through all one of the most constant of the members of the government in his attendance; one of the most hopeful in his views of the future of the school; ever a wise counsellor and a steadfast ally.

I could wish, how heartily I do wish it I cannot say, that the first President of the Institute of Technology, the illustrious Rogers, stood here in this place, on this occasion, to tell how much he and his colleagues were indebted to our venerable friend for his services in the inception and development of the Institute of Technology. But since that stately and gracious presence has passed away, it becomes the duty of his successor in office, though not in merit or in fame, to respond to this sentiment, and in behalf of the Corporation and the Faculty, to tender thanks and good wishes to the Hon. Marshall P. Wilder.

M. Denman Ross, Esq., in behalf of the Massachusetts
Institute of Technology, responded as follows : —

There are in the city of Boston several institutions
which owe their existence almost wholly to a band of
workers who have been for the past quarter of a century laboring to build them up solely for the public
good.   Mr. Wilder has been among the foremost of
this band.   He is a man "born to lead and command."   In all the enterprises of the day in which
he has taken a part, his fertile genius has been invoked, and has greatly characterized the matter in
hand.

About the year 1857 there was a movement in the
city of Boston to increase the facilities of the Boston
Society of Natural History, and to create a Polytechnic
and a Fine Art Institute.   The Massachusetts Horticultural Society was also seeking to find space for
a home.   I was a member of a self-constituted committee representing the several interests referred to,
who called on Governor Banks, and we asked him
to give us his co-operation in influencing the Legislature then in session to set apart, or reserve from
sale, about twenty acres of the space on the Back Bay
in the city of Boston.   I say space instead of land,
for the reason that what is now the most beautiful

part of the city was then covered with water, in many
places twenty feet deep. Our purpose was to secure
ample space for the educational institutions which the
committee represented, the most prominent at that
time being the proposed Polytechnic Institute, now
called the Massachusetts Institute of Technology.
Governor Banks asked us what axe we had to grind,
and our reply was, " The broad-axe of the State of
Massachusetts, your Excellency ; and we want you
with the Legislature to turn the grindstone."

Our zeal was somewhat chilled, but we were not dis-
couraged by the Governor's somewhat adverse attitude.
We soon discovered that the work we had in hand
required a permanent organization of our volunteer
committee ; and in our search for a leader Marshall
P. Wilder was pointed out to us as the man of all
others to swing the long-handled broad-axe of the
State, and direct the attention of the Legislature to
the justness of the cause we represented.   It was
not difficult to persuade him to be the chairman of
the so-called Back Bay Reservation Committee, and
his quick perception of the great future of this
movement enabled him to broaden our plans.   His
strong faith in the importance of the project inspired
us to call again to inform his Excellency of our
determination to persevere ; and not unlike the coon
which began to descend from the tree and surrender
as soon as he saw that David Crockett was pointing

his gun, the Governor surrendered, but exclaimed, "What a mistake! Mr. Wilder will, unless we check him, cover the whole Back Bay with an Agricultural College and warehouses for his specimens in Pomology, which he will call Museums."

Our leader never hesitated, although it required four years to convince the Legislature of the importance of our cause; but Mr. Wilder's magnetic power helped to enlist such men as Governor Andrew, Professor Wm. B. Rogers, and others. He worked, and others worked, and the effort was crowned with success.

Mr. Wilder's characteristic talent and persistent loyalty to the cause have been among the strongest elements of success in all that has been done in building up for the last quarter of a century the educational institutions on the Back Bay. I will name among those coming directly under his creative influence the Massachusetts Institute of Technology and the Boston Society of Natural History. The success attending these institutions led to building up others; and now we have the Boston Museum of Fine Arts, the Harvard Medical School, the Young Men's Christian Association, the Mechanics and Manufacturers' Institute, and the Mechanics' Charitable Association. We shall soon have the Boston Public Library and many more schools of general usefulness. Millions of money have been raised and invested for public education, which could only have been done by the inspiration of such men as Mr. Wilder. He is universally recognized as one of the foremost of the standard-bearers in all this great educational movement; and one evidence of the vitality of this educational current is the quarter of a million of dollars which has been raised as a memorial fund in honor of the late Professor William B. Rogers, the first President of the Massachusetts Institute of Technology. Mr. Wilder has been from the organization of this institution a constant attendant on the meetings of the Government; and to this day his venerable presence encourages and animates deliberation.

My purpose, Mr. President, and Gentlemen, in calling your attention to what seems to me to be wanting as a link in the history of the life of our honored friend, is simply that you may be led to look further for the foot-prints of Mr. Wilder; and in so doing you will see the wonderful influence which a single man exercises, when he takes hold of the broad-axes of a State like the one in which we live.

The Hon. EDWARD S. TOBEY, the Postmaster of Boston, was called upon, and responded as follows : —

Mr. PRESIDENT, — You are aware that no intimation whatever has been made that any remarks would be expected from me on this occasion; and when I found myself most agreeably placed at table between two distinguished Federal officers, I ventured to presume that the audience might be spared the infliction of a speech by me. But I beg to assure you that I esteem it both an honor and a privilege to participate with others in this highly appropriate recognition of the public services and personal worth of our venerable friend and guest.

I was gratified to hear him give special prominence to his position and influence as a merchant, in comparison with his official connection with very many of the noble, philanthropic, and educational institutions of our State and city, and trace his ability to aid in sustaining them to the pecuniary resources derived from his mercantile business: a fact, as you are aware, not uncommon in the experience of other merchants.

Our professional friends who are present, will, I trust, pardon me if I venture to assume that, to be an intelligent and successful merchant in conducting

certain important branches of business on an extended
scale, requires ability equal at least to that demanded
by either of the so-called learned professions.   The
lawyer argues his client's case, while the responsibility
of its decision and its consequences rest with either
the judge, or the jury, or both; and whatever the
result, whether adverse or otherwise, his fee is secure.
The merchant must gather his facts often too super-
ficially, make his logical deductions, and arrive at
a decision in the silent operations of the mind, to
be carried into effect so promptly that it may cost
him in some instances the loss of half, or possibly the
whole, of his fortune.   Such are the vicissitudes of a
business life, that a very small per cent of those who
engage in it escape failure sooner or later, and possibly the loss of the accumulations of a lifetime.   We
may therefore the more cordially congratulate our
venerable friend, Colonel Wilder, as being one of the
few whose successful experience has followed him
so near to the closing years of a long and arduous
life.

Merchants are, and always have been, especially
prominent in founding, as well as in supporting by
their liberal benefactions, philanthropic and educational institutions, as well as in relieving the wants
of their less favored fellow-men.   They are also, as
is well known, the generous patrons of the fine arts.
With all these great public interests, Colonel Wilder

has ever been identified, and with an assiduity so
remarkable as to suggest the impression that he has
long acted under the belief which may well animate
each of us, that no life can be pleasing to God that
is not useful to man.

AARON H. BEAN, Esq., President of the Hamilton Bank, was called upon, and spoke as follows : —

Mr. PRESIDENT, and GENTLEMEN, — It is with great pleasure that I respond to your call. You have referred to the Hamilton Bank as one of the institutions with which our honored guest has been long connected. The Bank was organized on the 13th day of February, 1832, and upon the first list of Directors appears the name of Marshall P. Wilder; and in that capacity he has served under its State and National organizations uninterruptedly for a period of nearly fifty-two years, and is the sole survivor of that distinguished Board of Boston merchants.

The Directors of the Hamilton National Bank, upon hearing that it was proposed by numerous friends to celebrate the eighty-fifth anniversary of the birthday of their senior associate, took early official action, and by a unanimous vote of the Board appointed the President and Messrs. S. S. Blanchard and Henry G. Denny a Committee to attend the festivities and join in the congratulations of the occasion.

With this official authority I stand here with my associates in the presence of this large company, to bear witness to the zeal and fidelity of our venerable friend in the discharge of his duty as a director of the Bank for more than half a century; and also to bear to him the congratulations of each member of the Board, that he is able on this, the eighty-fifth anniversary of his birthday, to meet around the festive board, with mental powers unimpaired, so many of his associates of earlier and later years, and also to assure him of their undiminished confidence and respect.

And, Sir, if I may be permitted to make a personal allusion, I wish thus publicly to thank our friend for the many kind words and acts with which he has cheered me in my various duties for a long period of years.

Mr. Chairman, as I was looking over the pages of a valued book a short time since, I read a sentence which now seems to me so appropriate to this occasion, that I venture to repeat it: —

" The oak-tree was once an acorn under the ground, then a little plant in the turf; now it stands aloft, a full-grown oak. So a good old age grows up to the height of thoughts not of this world. It is always shedding ripe fruits, and every beholder is the better even for looking at it."

Benjamin F. Stevens, Esq., President of the New England Mutual Life Insurance Company, responded as follows : —

Mr. President, and Gentlemen, — I do not know that I can say anything in addition to what has been said of the distinguished gentleman whose birthday we are honoring this evening; but I desire to add my tribute to the value of his great public as well as private services to the community during a period of more than half a century of active industrial life. The world knows that Marshall P. Wilder has been a moving spirit in whatever he has undertaken, especially in developing and maturing the great agricultural interests of the country ; at the same time following a commercial career, fairly earning therein the reputation of " an honorable and upright merchant."

To have been connected with Colonel Wilder in the management of the New England Mutual Life Insurance Company, in which he has been a director for nearly forty years, is to me a pleasurable record. He has followed the fortunes of that institution through infancy, youth, and mature age, as a member of its finance and other sub-committees of its trustees.

If I were to suggest a sentiment, Mr. Chairman, it would be that our friend and counsellor, our Nestor, may enjoy the period of life allotted to him, and continue to be as he ever has been, a "man of the people."

The Hon. CHARLES R. TRAIN, a Director of the Home Savings Bank, responded as follows : —

Mr. PRESIDENT, — When Lafayette visited New England, and assisted in laying the corner-stone of the Bunker Hill Monument, I was present, a child in my father's arms. Young as I was, I well remember the appearance of the nation's guest, and the astonishing enthusiasm with which he was greeted, as at the bidding of the matchless orator of the occasion he arose and bowed his emotions to that vast congregation. It was a lesson never to be forgotten, teaching the measure of a people's appreciation of great public service, and the value of a manhood compacted with usefulness, integrity, and honor.

Our guest to-night was at that time in the early blossom of a vigorous manhood, and now bears with him substantially the memories of this century. His growth, to borrow an idea, has not been like that of the poplar and other rapidly growing trees, but like that of the oak, in a period of eighty-five years outstripping them all, maintaining its dignity, and dispensing its blessings to a grateful nation.

For thirty years I have enjoyed his society and been benefited by his counsels, and in common with all our people have learned to love and venerate him as a friend, to esteem him as a public benefactor, to feel his presence a blessing and his advice a benediction. But it is not of his character, influenced by the peculiar tastes which he has so successfully cultivated, and which have given him such a world-wide reputation, that I wish to speak, but of his faithfulness in every relation which he has held to his fellow-men. Let me speak of one, of which I know whereof I affirm.

In February, 1870, the Home Savings Bank was organized, with Colonel Wilder as its first Vice-President: a position which he has held in storm and sunshine ever since. We were told by the older banks in the city that if our deposits were one hundred thousand dollars at the end of the first year we should do well. At the close of that year we had received and invested a little over one million dollars. I need not say to this audience how much of the confidence of the public in this institution was due to the fact that Colonel Wilder was a working and not an ornamental officer. In six years we had accumulated over seven millions of dollars. When the storm came which wrecked so many of our savings banks, the Home, through the hostility of an individual then connected with the public press, but for several years past, and now, a fugitive from justice, was placed in the van, and received the first shock of the crisis. Colonel Wilder, thoroughly acquainted with the condition of the Bank, was instant, in season and out of season, in attendance upon his duties; and many of the depositors have lived to bless him for his sympathy in their distress, and for the sound advice by following which their little all was preserved.

Thanks to Colonel Wilder and his associates, the Bank survived; and its books show that in the thirteen years of its life it has received over eighteen millions of deposits, has paid out about two millions in dividends, averaging $5\frac{40}{100}$ per cent, and that no depositor has suffered a loss by any misconduct of the Bank; and it has to-day a deposit of nearly two millions, and a surplus of over two hundred and thirty-one thousand dollars. All this is due to the faithful and persistent labors of Colonel Wilder and his colleagues; and in behalf of the Trustees, and of the poor people who have been benefited thereby, I present to him the assurance of our profoundest gratitude.

Such services as these, the only reward for which is the consciousness of well-doing, entitle our guest to have his name enrolled with the public benefactors of the State.

WILLIAM D. COOLIDGE, Esq., Past Grand Master of the Grand Lodge of Freemasons of Massachusetts, spoke as follows : —

Mr. PRESIDENT, and GENTLEMEN, — I desire to say a few words to my dear friend and brother, our honored guest. I will only detain you a few moments, to express my happiness in being with you on this occasion, uniting most heartily in every expression of appreciation and affection which has been uttered ; they have been as numerous as the varied positions which you have filled so fully and so usefully in a long and eventful life.

This has been a most fitting, sincere, and merited tribute ; because in you were found the warm heart and the active will to use the means and ability with which God has blessed you, to benefit your fellow-men and the age in which we live, making you the instrument in his hands of lasting benefit to the race, inspiring them with the priceless "love of the beautiful."

My Brother, our business relations have not called us much together ; but it has been my happy privilege to meet you with loving friends in the sacred retirement of your beautiful home, where filial affection and devoted love and care crowned your happiness, and met the ready response of the loving and devoted husband and father. But I must not dwell on this, and I only speak of it as the crowning glory of a complete life.

My Brother, when in 1860, by the partial love and confidence of my brethren, I was elected Grand Master of Masons in Massachusetts, it became my duty to select from among them one who united consummate judgment with a wise discretion and executive ability, to fill the office of Deputy Grand Master; and as my confidential counsellor and adviser, you did me and the Grand Lodge of Massachusetts the honor to accept that appointment in the trying period of the opening of the late war, and you won for yourself their lasting respect and brotherly affection. And so, my Brother, I bring to you to-night the congratulations of the whole Fraternity in Massachusetts, and their best wishes for the continuance of that happiness to yourself which you have so liberally bestowed on others, and which a grateful community acknowledges. I close these remarks with my own sincere wish that your valuable life may be continued in comfort and happiness till the message is sent to " come up higher."

The Hon. CHARLES L. FLINT, of the Massachusetts Agricultural Club, responded as follows: —

Mr. PRESIDENT, and GENTLEMEN, — It hardly becomes me, being about the youngest of the jolly set of boys known as the Massachusetts Agricultural Club, to presume to speak as their representative.

It is now nearly forty-four years since a " picked company," the leaders of men in horticultural and agricultural pursuits, appreciating the charms as well as the solid advantages of social intercourse, met to lay the foundations of this distinguished Club. Colonel Wilder and the genial and popular proprietor of the celebrated Weld Farm are the only survivors of the choice spirits who met around that social and festive board. Now, the members of that Club are more familiar, perhaps, with the inner life, the buoyant and indomitable spirits of their President, and the graceful and jaunty way in which he wears the mantle of old age, than some others who see him from a greater distance. We sit by his side, listen to his perennial wit and his sparkling and ready repartees, till it becomes rather difficult to realize that he is anything but a boy like ourselves.

To be sure, we appreciate his record, and take the greatest delight in recounting his brilliant and honor-

able achievements; that is how he came to be chosen
as our leader. The boys all saw that few men in
our community had made a more striking or a more
durable mark than Colonel Wilder; that few had held
more important public positions or sustained themselves more honorably in them, through so long a
course of years; that it had fallen to the lot of few
of their comrades to initiate so many beneficent public enterprises which have enured to the welfare of
the people among whom they have lived.

Well, Sir, we think we have done something to
preserve his youthful freshness, and to keep alive
his keen relish for the social side of life; and that,
I take it, is the real secret of a happy, a cheerful,
and a delightful old age.

I recollect that many years since I had to read and
study two charming essays, written nearly two thousand years ago by Cicero, the renowned, the eloquent
and silver-tongued orator and statesman of Rome,
one upon Friendship, the other upon Old Age; and
the sweet and genial philosophy of those papers has
been something of a consolation to me all my life.
What is there in the poetry or the prose of man's life
on earth more lovely or more charming than a quiet,
contented, and dignified old age, cheered by the
friendship of the wise and good? And why should
any rational or sensible being dread the approach of
old age, or try to hide from himself or others that he

is advanced in years? If goodness has crowned his days, and the harvests of successive years have been garnered in the mind as a well-filled storehouse, and the love of children and grandchildren throws its arms around him or climbs his knees "the envied kiss to share," and hope opens the portals of heaven on his vision, and his soul is at peace, like a foretaste of the rest that awaits him at the end of his pilgrimage, why should not old age be the happiest, the loveliest, the cosiest season of the life on earth? We are apt to forget that the heart never grows old, and that out of the heart are the issues of life. The soul never grows old, and the soul is the man. We know that this mortal frame of ours is not the thing that is to be, and not even the thing that is, if we are to judge by the power to be, to do, to suffer, and to enjoy; for we know that the real life of man is the soul, and that that is what loves, learns, hopes, rejoices in the smile of God and friends, and lives the most when it is freed from these trammels of the body.

We all recognize Colonel Wilder as a prominent public benefactor. If he had done nothing more than to introduce many new fruits and flowers, and to multiply new varieties by hybridization, he would have laid the community under great obligations to him. But his range of activity has been far wider. A large part of the beauty, the cultured taste and the luxuriance of landscape gardening that clusters around and adorns the thousands of homesteads about Boston, through a constantly widening radius, is due directly or indirectly to his influence and inspiration. And now, at the venerable age of eighty-five, from the quiet retreat of his happy home, he can look back upon a long life well spent, and out upon a region smiling with loveliness, with a consciousness that he is surrounded by a host of admiring and devoted friends who realize and appreciate the results of his labors and the powerful impetus which his personal presence gave to the spirit of improvement, thirty, forty, fifty years ago.

On behalf of the Agricultural Club, we wish him still many more years of happiness and useful activity.

NOTE.—Messrs. FRANCIS A. WALKER, M. DENMAN ROSS, CHARLES L. FLINT, BENJAMIN F. STEVENS, and CHARLES R. TRAIN were unable to remain until the end of the Banquet, and kindly sent to the Committee the substance of what they intended to say, as reported in preceding pages.

At the conclusion of the speaking, the company rose, and as a parting ceremony sang the following lines from Burns's song of Auld Lang Syne: —

"Should auld acquaintance be forgot,
And never brought to min'?
Should auld acquaintance be forgot,
And days o' lang syne?
For auld lang syne, my dear,
For auld lang syne,
We 'll tak' a cup o' kindness yet,
For auld lang syne.

"And here 's a hand, my trusty fier,
And gie 's a hand o' thine;
And we 'll tak' a right guid-willie waught,
For auld lang syne.
For auld lang syne, my dear,
For auld lang syne,
We 'll tak' a cup o' kindness yet,
For auld lang syne."

LETTER OF INVITATION.

AT the suggestion of numerous friends, a Dinner in honor of the Hon. MARSHALL P. WILDER, to celebrate the anniversary of his eighty-fifth birthday, will be given at the Parker House, September 22d, at 3 o'clock P. M., at which you are cordially invited to be present.

CHAS. H. B. BRECK, ⎫
JOHN C. HOVEY, ⎬ *Committee.*
ROBERT MANNING, ⎭

LETTERS IN REPLY TO THE INVITATION OF THE COMMITTEE.

Letter of the Hon. Robert C. Winthrop.

BROOKLINE, MASS., 17th Sept., 1883.

DEAR SIR, — Your obliging invitation of the 10th inst. has awaited my return from a visit to my grand-children at Lenox. I thank you for including me among those who would gladly pay a tribute of re-spect to our excellent friend, Marshall P. Wilder, on his eighty-fifth birthday. I have known him inti-mately for a full half of his long pilgrimage, and every year has added to my impressions of his ability and usefulness. His services to Horticulture and Agriculture have been invaluable. No other man has done so much for our fields and gardens and orchards. He has distinguished himself in many other lines of life, and his relations to the Legisla-ture of Massachusetts and to the Historic Genealog-ical Society will not soon be forgotten. But his name will have its most enduring and most enviable association with the flowers and fruits for whose cul-ture he was foremost in striving, both by precept and example. He deserves a grateful remembrance as

long as a fine pear is relished or a brilliant bouquet
admired.

I regret that it will not be in my power to be with
you and with him on the 22d inst., and can only beg
you to offer him my hearty congratulations on the
occasion.

Believe me, dear sir, respectfully and truly yours,

ROBERT C. WINTHROP.

C. H. B. BRECK, Esq.

---

*Letter of his Excellency, Benjamin F. Butler, Governor of
Massachusetts.*

COMMONWEALTH OF MASSACHUSETTS,
EXECUTIVE DEPARTMENT,

BOSTON, Sept. 15, 1883.

DEAR SIR, — I have the honor to acknowledge
your courteous invitation to attend a dinner on the
occasion of the remembrance of the eighty-fifth
birthday of the Hon. Marshall P. Wilder.

How deeply I regret that I cannot be present, you
will see from the fact —

First, that he is a citizen of New Hampshire;
that he, with myself, came to Massachusetts from
New Hampshire, and we New Hampshire men are
somewhat clannish.

Second, from my admiration for his long and useful life; for the labors to which we owe very many

of the substantial improvements in the agricultural condition of Massachusetts.

Third, he has sustained by his efforts and fostering care the Massachusetts Agricultural Society.

Lastly, and above all, for the admiration I have, and should be glad to testify, to a man of sterling integrity and of culture, who now has reason to rejoice in the appreciation of all his fellow-citizens for his industrious, noble, and well-spent life.

A previous engagement away from Boston, which cannot well be shunned or avoided, renders my presence impossible; which your honored guest will pardon to me, I am sure, because it is in the interest of agriculture.

Give him my deepest sensibilities, and believe me, personally,

Very truly yours,

BENJAMIN F. BUTLER.

CHAS. H. B. BRECK, Esq., Boston, Mass.

Letter of the Hon. George B. Loring, United States Commissioner of the Department of Agriculture.

SALEM, Sept. 13, 1883.

MY DEAR MR. BRECK, — I regret that engagements which I cannot avoid or postpone will prevent my accepting your polite invitation to the dinner to be given on the 22d inst., to celebrate the anniversary of the eighty-fifth birthday of the Hon. Marshall P. Wilder. Colonel Wilder's career, from his youth to the venerable old age which endears him to all who know him, has been so useful and honorable that not his friends only, but the entire community in which he lives may well pay him a full tribute of respect and admiration.   It is with pride and satisfaction that the business associations of the city of Boston can point to him as a representative of that mercantile integrity which gives that city its distinguished position among the great commercial centres of the world.   His early intimate association with those powerful and distinguished men who have given a lustre to Massachusetts which no attacks have yet bedimmed, cannot be forgotten by those who hold dear the names of Webster and Everett, and their distinguished associates, who always came at his call to encourage and elevate the great industry to which he has devoted all his leisure hours.   As the pioneer in all the most beautiful and elaborate modes of cultivation, by which the earth has brought forth an abundant harvest of whatever gratifies man's most refined tastes, he will always be held dear so long as the flowers of the garden, and the choicest fruits of the vineyard and the orchard add their beauty and luxuriance to our homes.

Not a public park, not a flower-garden, not an orchard, not a field of small fruits, not a vineyard, but bears the marks of his untiring efforts for every horticultural improvement known to us, and of his devotion to the pomological development of our country.

His devoted labor for the development of American agriculture formed of itself one of the most interesting chapters in the history of that important industry. When he began his work of encouraging the farmer in his toil, agriculture was in a primitive condition everywhere, and confined, in this country, to comparatively circumscribed limits. In Massachusetts the influence of a few liberal and energetic societies had been sensibly felt, it is true, and the introduction of improved machinery and new and valuable crops had met with hearty encouragement. But neither for Massachusetts nor for that widespread agricultural region from which are now drawn the great supplies for our home market and the main support of our foreign commerce, had any adequate system of tillage and harvesting been adopted; nor had the public mind been roused to a full understanding of the importance of a well-educated, scientific management of land, and a well-conducted increase and care of our flocks and herds. The great inventions of agricultural machinery which make the special farming of the East profitable and the wholesale farming of the West possible, were but just commenced, and had hardly made a step towards their present state of perfection. The whole system of agricultural education and investigation as now conducted was unknown. There was not an agricultural college in existence, boards of agriculture were unknown, the United States Department of Agriculture was not thought of. It was at this time that Colonel Wilder entered upon his judicious and earnest advocacy of agricultural improvement and progress. Every inventor found in him an encouraging friend. As President of the United States Agricultural Society his influence was felt throughout the length and breadth of the land. By his persuasion the State of Massachusetts was induced to organize and endow her State Board of Agriculture, whose long career has won the respect of all men, and whose effect has been universally felt. And to him, of all men in this Commonwealth, we are indebted for the establishment of a well-organized Agricultural College, almost the pioneer in these institutions, and whose educational work has been diligently and wisely pursued. There have been many enthusiastic and devoted friends of agriculture in this country, but there has been no one man who has exercised so long-continued, untiring, and inspiring influence as has Colonel Wilder. His name is connected with the choicest products of our soil, and will be remembered so long as man's love of nature, and her wonderful luxuriance and beauty shall endure. His memory will be cherished by all who realize that one of our highest duties is to adorn and beautify our homes, and by all who look upon a long and honorable life crowned with a happy old age as one of the most precious gifts bestowed upon man.

Truly your friend and servant,

GEORGE B. LORING.

CHAS. H. B. BRECK, Esq., Boston.

Letter of the Hon. William Claflin, Ex-Governor of Massachusetts.

BOSTON, Sept. 22, 1883.

MY DEAR SIR, — It is with sincere regret that I am obliged to decline the very kind invitation of the Committee to join your many friends in congratulating you upon the return of your birthday.

It is allotted to few men to greet the morning sun at the age of eighty-five ; and to fewer still, in comfortable health, to gather at the social board their associates in business, in society, in church, and in those public enterprises which tend to build up a community in its noblest and most enduring form.

For half a century your name has given strength to the best aspirations of the people, and your presence has been welcomed by the trusted leaders of public opinion in their deliberations for the general welfare. The retrospect must be most gratifying as

you survey the wonderful events through which you
have passed, and remember the distinguished men
who have been your companions in public and
private life.   Be assured that those who meet you
on this glad occasion represent the general feeling of
the people of the State, in their appreciation of your
personal worth and your devotion to the high trusts
committed to your care.   Your friends everywhere
rejoice in your lengthened life, and trust that many
years may be added to it, enabling you to gladden
their hearts often by your cheerful presence and wise
counsel.

With sincere thanks for your remembrance on this,
as well as on many other occasions of the deepest
interest, I am

Your friend and servant,

WILLIAM CLAFLIN.

The Hon. MARSHALL P. WILDER.

---

*Letter of the Hon. John D. Long, Ex-Governor of
Massachusetts.*

HINGHAM, Sept. 11, 1883.

DEAR MR. BRECK, — My engagements prevent my
attending the dinner to be given to Mr. Wilder on the
22d inst., but I cannot forbear to express my great
respect for him, my appreciation of his long and
honorable life, and my good wishes for its happy
and honored continuance.   He has adorned the

Commonwealth in many positions and rendered her useful and beneficent service. I can think of no more gratifying spectacle than such a noble old age, ripe and sweet and fair as the autumn fruits to the perfection of which he has so greatly contributed.

Very truly yours,

JOHN D. LONG.

Letter of the Hon. Thomas Talbot, Ex-Governor of Massachusetts.

BILLERICA, Sept. 18, 1883.

DEAR SIR, — I regret that I cannot be present at the interesting anniversary to which you refer in your invitation of the 10th inst. A business connection of more than a quarter of a century has led me to have a high respect and regard for the recipient of your kindness on the present occasion.

The great public services of the Hon. Marshall P. Wilder, especially in regard to the development of the agricultural and horticultural interests of the country, should pass his name down to posterity as a public benefactor whose great services are remembered with gratitude by the State and Nation.

May many anniversaries come and go before he is called to his reward!

Yours very truly,

THOMAS TALBOT.

CHAS. H. B. BRECK, Esq.

Letter of Oliver Wendell Holmes, M. D.

BEVERLY FARMS, MASS., Sept. 14, 1883.

MY DEAR SIR, — I am sorry that it will not be in my power to be present at the dinner to be given on the 22d, to celebrate the eighty-fifth birthday of the Hon. Marshall P. Wilder.

As to the "few lines" you are pleased to suggest, I must remind you that I consider myself an *Emeritus* in that line of business, as well as an Emeritus Professor; not for the merit of any lines I may have written, but for the number of them. But my heart is always on duty, and it prompts me to send my best and warmest wishes to the venerable and venerated friend who has outlived the fruits of four-score seasons, and is still ripening as if his life were all summer.

Believe me, dear sir, very truly yours,

O. W. HOLMES.

CHARLES H. B. BRECK, Esq.

Letter of the Hon. Martin P. Kennard, Assistant Treasurer of the United States at Boston.

BROOKLINE, Sept. 21, 1883.

DEAR SIR, — I seriously regret that an imperative claim upon me elsewhere will deprive me of the pleasure of joining in your graceful compliment to the

Hon. Marshall P. Wilder. My recollections of his mercantile prominence, his probity, his ever active public spirit, his patriotism, and his *pears*, run back to my juvenile days. And I especially regret my absence as I recall his agreeable personality during fifteen years of my own active business life, when with a small suburban coterie, who were compelled regularly to dine in town, through hard times and through war-times, he presided at the table spread for us, always entertaining, always happy, and *all-ways* Christian, "with kindness for all, with malice towards none." Nine of these years we met at the old Bromfield House, and six of them at the Tremont. Franklin Pierce, John A. Andrew, Isaac O. Barnes, George S. Hillard, Caleb Cushing, David Nevins, James T. Fields, Waldo Maynard, Selden Crockett, who have passed beyond the curtain, and many others as well known, both of the living and the dead, were then sometimes there with us; and at your table to-morrow the pleasant aroma of those memories will surely mingle with that of your flowers and your laurels. I beg to offer my best wishes for the occasion, and invoke for our venerable guest still many years of felicity, unclouded by infirmity or by sorrow.

Faithfully yours,

M. P. KENNARD.

C. H. B. BRECK, Esq., Chairman.

*Letter of the Hon. Francis W. Bird, President of
the Bird Club.*

EAST WALPOLE, NOV. 30, 1883.

DEAR SIR, — I regret that I was obliged to leave
the hall early when the friends of the Hon. Marshall
P. Wilder were celebrating the eighty-fifth anniversary of his birth. I should have been glad to say
a few words there in testimony of my high regard
for my ancient friend, and of my admiration for his
valuable services to various good causes during a
long life.

I flatter myself that I have a special right to
speak in praise of Colonel Wilder's public work
for nearly forty years; for I think I had a good
deal to do with preventing his entering political
life instead of engaging in those departments in
which he has been so eminently useful. After a
sharp contest in the Whig legislative caucus in 1848,
Edward L. Keyes, of Dedham, was nominated over
Colonel Wilder, as Executive Councillor; and after
an equally sharp contest in the legislative convention, Mr. Keyes was elected. I am afraid that my
personal relations with my brilliant but erratic friend
Keyes controlled my action, rather than regard for the
public welfare. The Commonwealth, my subsequent

acquaintance with Colonel Wilder has taught me, lost
a good Councillor; perhaps his defeat tended to give
to the agricultural interests a rare benefactor.

Those who have been intimately associated with
Colonel Wilder can speak far more intelligently of
his great services in the department of Agriculture
than I can; but I can speak, and take pleasure in
speaking, of what he has done for so many years to
promote good fellowship. As the father of the Massachusetts Agricultural Club, at the head of whose
weekly gatherings he has sat for so many years, he
has brought together a large circle of educated and
practical agriculturalists; and while the discussions at
those dinners would naturally be largely connected
with agricultural topics, yet to my mind, and I doubt
not in the experience of those gentlemen, a great,
I think I might say the greatest, benefit of the association has been in the personal friendships it has
cultivated.

Comparing Colonel Wilder's achievements in the
fields to which he has devoted his life with the records of those who entered public life thirty-five years
ago, it is safe to say that his labors in behalf of the
cultivators of farm, garden, and orchard have far
overshadowed in their beneficent results all that has
been done by any score of the average politicians of
that day; and that he will be freshly remembered by
his associates of the Agricultural Club long after the

politicians are forgotten.   To our friend himself the
memories of his long and useful life must cheer his
days as the sun goes down ; for as Jeanie Deans so
eloquently says: "When the hour of death comes,
that comes to high and low, lang and late may it
be his! then it isna what we hae dune for oursels,
but what we hae dune for others, that we think on
maist pleasantly."

And thus, in view of the beneficent life of our
venerable friend, and of the serene evening so well
befitting its close, we have the right to address to
him the words of Emerson : —

> Lowly faithful, banish fear ;
>   Right onward drive, unharmed.
> The port, well worth the cruise, is near,
>   And every wave is charmed.

Very truly yours,

F. W. BIRD.

C. H. B. BRECK, Esq.

Letter of the Hon. Charles Levi Woodbury.

BOSTON, Sept. 19, 1883.

GENTLEMEN, — It would give me the greatest pleasure to join in the festival to the Hon. Marshall P.
Wilder, but I shall leave town that day for the West,
and cannot be present.

I regret this personally, because I should like to
be a party with his numerous friends in testifying

the results of a long acquaintance with the gentleman who will be your guest. It would be more
gratifying to his modesty that these things should
not be said to his face, but to you; and behind his
back I feel bold enough to say that although when
I first knew him he was as old as I now am, and
therefore entitled to the deference due to seniority,
yet that has only made me appreciate with keener
obligation the sincerity and frankness which, equally
with the scope of his attainments and the vigorous
grasp of his intellect, have made his friendship a
source of pleasure and an exhaustless mine for
instruction and wisdom.

I should indeed love to grasp him by the hand,
look into his kindly beaming eyes on this occasion,
and gaze on his stalwart and vigorous figure; and I
should not now write as much were it not that his
health seems to have been drawn from a fountain
of perpetual youth; and he appears so likely to out-
live me that, to use an Irishism, I fear I shall never
live to make a funeral oration over him unless I do
it now. Unlike the century-plant which blossoms
only once in a hundred years, he blossoms for a
hundred years at a time; and what then?

Give him for me the right hand of fellowship, and
believe me

Sincerely yours, and his,

CHARLES LEVI WOODBURY.

CHAS. H. B. BRECK, Esq.

Letter of the Hon. Frederic W. Lincoln, Ex-Mayor of the City of Boston.

BOSTON, Sept. 17, 1883.

DEAR SIR, — I regret that an engagement on the afternoon of the 22d inst. will prevent my acceptance of the courteous invitation to be present at the complimentary dinner to the Hon. Marshall P. Wilder.

His long and valued services to this community certainly deserve recognition. In everything that marks the citizen and the man his career has been pre-eminent, and his friends do well to unite in a social and in somewhat semi-official way, in congratulations upon the happy recurrence of the eighty-fifth anniversary of his birth.

Will you please tender to Mr. Wilder my personal congratulations, and believe me to be

Yours very truly,

F. W. LINCOLN.

CHAS. H. B. BRECK, Esq.

Letter of the Rev. James H. Means, D. D.

DORCHESTER, Sept. 13, 1883.

MY DEAR SIR, — I have had the honor of receiving your invitation to the celebration of the eighty-fifth anniversary of the birth of my parishioner and friend,

Colonel Wilder. My regard for him, his constant kindness to me, and my admiration of a life so prolonged, yet filled up with activity to the end, combine to make me desirous of joining you and your friends on that occasion; but the state of my health obliges me to be absent.

Please, therefore, accept my thanks for your courtesy, and believe me,

Cordially yours,

J. H. Means.

The Hon. C. H. B. Breck.

Letter of Mr. C. M. Atkinson, a professional gardener.

Brookline, Sept. 22, 1883.

Dear Sir, — I regret that I cannot be one of your gathering, to offer congratulations to our noble captain. It is given but to few to attain to fourscore-and-five years, and those not of labor and sorrow, but of joyful usefulness. It is given but to few to gather around such a noble chieftain and offer their heart-felt congratulations; and in doing so we do not honor him as much as we do ourselves.

His desire for the good of his fellow-men is as broad as this broad continent. The natural good and the moral good in him do but find an echo, thrilling and animating each according to the measure of good vouchsafed to him. A life so well rounded, so full of usefulness and earnest desire to impart beauty, luxury, and joy equally to the humble cot and the proud palace, can no more die than beauty or music. The brightness of its memory may fade, but it will be deathless.

So long as orchards are planted, gardens cultivated, and flowers associated with all our joys and all our sorrows, so long will the name of Wilder live.

I am, my dear sir,

Ever truly yours,

C. M. ATKINSON.

NAMES OF THE GENTLEMEN

WHO PARTICIPATED IN THE BANQUET GIVEN TO THE
HON. MARSHALL P. WILDER, ON THE EIGHTY-
FIFTH ANNIVERSARY OF HIS BIRTHDAY,
SEPTEMBER 22, 1883.

The Hon. MARSHALL PINCKNEY WILDER, Ph. D., the honored
guest of the occasion.

The Hon. CHARLES H. B. BRECK, Vice-President of the Massachusetts Horticultural Society, and Chairman of the Committee
of Arrangements.

The Rev. GEORGE W. BLAGDEN, D.D., *Minister Emeritus* of the
Old South Church, Boston.

His Honor OLIVER AMES, Lieutenant-Governor of Massachusetts.

His Honor ALBERT PALMER, Mayor of Boston.

The Hon. ALEXANDER H. RICE, Ex-Governor of Massachusetts,
and Trustee of the Massachusetts Institute of Technology.

The Hon. JOSHUA L. CHAMBERLAIN, late President of Bowdoin College, and Ex-Governor of Maine.

The Hon. FREDERICK SMYTH, Vice-President of the United States
Agricultural Society, and Ex-Governor of New Hampshire.

The Hon. LEVERETT SALTONSTALL, Vice-President of the Massachusetts Society for the Promotion of Agriculture.

The Hon. FRANCIS B. HAYES, President of the Massachusetts Horticultural Society.

Pres. J. C. GREENOUGH, President of the Massachusetts Agricultural
College.

General NATHANIEL P. BANKS, United States Marshal and Ex-
Governor of Massachusetts.

The Rev. EDWARD N. PACKARD, Pastor of the Second Church, Dorchester.

Major BEN: PERLEY POORE, Past Commander of the Ancient and Honorable Artillery Company, and Secretary of the United States Agricultural Society.

The Hon. JOHN CUMMINGS, President of the Middlesex Agricultural Society, and Treasurer of the Massachusetts Agricultural College.

The Hon. EDWARD S. TOBEY, Postmaster of Boston.

The Hon. GEORGE P. SANGER, United States District Attorney.

The Hon. FRANCIS W. BIRD, President of the Bird Club.

The Hon. WILLIAM S. GARDNER, Justice of the Superior Court.

The Hon. JOHN M. CLARK, Sheriff of Suffolk.

The Hon. GEORGE C. RICHARDSON, Vice-President of the New England Historic Genealogical Society.

The Rev. EDMUND F. SLAFTER, Corresponding Secretary of the New England Historic Genealogical Society.

BENJAMIN B. TORREY, Esq., Treasurer of the New England Historic Genealogical Society.

The Rev. INCREASE N. TARBOX, D.D., Historiographer of the New England Historic Genealogical Society.

The Hon. NATHANIEL F. SAFFORD, Director in the New England Historic Genealogical Society.

DAVID GREENE HASKINS, JR., Esq., Recording Secretary of the New England Historic Genealogical Society.

JOHN WARD DEAN, Esq., Librarian of the New England Historic Genealogical Society, and Editor of the Historical and Genealogical Register.

The Hon. FRANCIS M. WELD, Vice-President of the Massachusetts Agricultural Club.

AARON DAVIS WELD, Esq., Member and one of the founders of the Massachusetts Agricultural Club.

HORATIO HOLLIS HUNNEWELL, Esq., Ex-Vice-president of the Massachusetts Horticultural Society and Member of the Massachusetts Agricultural Club.

The HON. CHARLES L. FLINT, Member of the Massachusetts Agricultural Club, and Ex-Secretary of the Massachusetts Board of Agriculture.

The Hon. JOHN E. RUSSELL, Secretary of the Massachusetts Board of Agriculture.

Dr. JOSEPH BURNETT, Member of the Massachusetts Agricultural Club.

JOHN GARDNER, Esq., Member of the Massachusetts Agricultural Club.

The Hon. STEPHEN M. ALLEN, Corresponding Secretary of the Webster Historical Society.

OAKES A. AMES, Esq., Member of the New England Historic Genealogical Society.

The Hon. JAMES S. GRINNELL, Trustee of the Massachusetts Agricultural College.

O. B. HADWEN, Esq., Trustee of the Massachusetts Agricultural College.

BENJAMIN P. WARE, Esq., President of the Essex Agricultural Society, and a Trustee of the Massachusetts Agricultural College.

The Hon. DANIEL NEEDHAM, Secretary of the New England Agricultural Society, and Trustee of the Massachusetts Agricultural College.

GEORGE NOYES, Esq., Editor of the Massachusetts Ploughman, and Trustee of the Massachusetts Agricultural College.

M. DENMAN ROSS, Esq., Trustee of the Massachusetts Institute of Technology.

AARON H. BEAN, Esq., President of the Hamilton Bank.

S. STODDARD BLANCHARD, Esq., Ex-President of the Hamilton Bank.

HENRY G. DENNY, Esq., Director of the Hamilton Bank.

Benjamin F. Stevens, Esq., President of the New England Mutual Life Insurance Company.

Joseph M. Gibbens, Secretary of the New England Mutual Life Insurance Company.

The Hon. Nathaniel J. Bradlee, President of the Massachusetts Charitable Mechanics' Association.

The Hon. Charles R. Train, late Attorney-General of Massachusetts and Trustee of the Home Savings Bank.

Samuel Atherton, Esq., Trustee of the Home Savings Bank.

William D. Coolidge, Esq., Past Grand-Master of the Massachusetts Grand Lodge of Freemasons.

F. Lyman Winship, of the Massachusetts Grand Lodge of Freemasons.

William G. Underwood, of the Massachusetts Grand Lodge of Freemasons.

Ezra Farnsworth, Esq., of the firm of Parker, Wilder, and Company.

Benjamin Phipps, Esq., of the firm of Parker, Wilder, and Company.

William H. Wilder, Esq., of the firm of Parker, Wilder, and Company.

The Rev. Luther Farnham, Librarian of the General Theological Library.

Dr. Henry P. Walcott, Member of the Massachusetts Board of Health.

Dr. Milbrey Green, Ex-President of Massachusetts Eclectic Medical Society.

Jonathan French, Esq., Member of the Massachusetts Horticultural Society.

Edward Whitney, Esq., Boston Merchant.

William Durant, Esq., of the Boston Evening Transcript.

Elbridge Torrey, Esq., Boston Merchant.

Henry C. Brooks, Esq., Boston Merchant.

DAVID B. FLINT, Esq., President of the Charles River Bank.

EBEN SNOW, Esq., Cashier of the Charles River Bank.

JOHN L. STEVENSON, Esq., President of the Boston Club.

FREDERIC W. G. MAY, Esq., Member of the Bostonian Society.

ALBERT MORSE, Esq., Boston Merchant.

WILLIAM G. SMITH, Esq., of the Massachusetts Horticultural Society.

JOHNSON CLARK, Esq., Member of the Massachusetts Horticultural Society.

JESSE C. IVY, Esq., Member of the Massachusetts Horticultural Society.

WILLIAM WALLACE, Esq., Boston Merchant.

WILLIAM H. WILDER, JR., Grandson of the Hon. MARSHALL P. WILDER.

CHARLES M. HOVEY, Esq., Ex-President of the Massachusetts Horticultural Society.

BENJAMIN G. SMITH, Esq., Vice-President of the Massachusetts Horticultural Society.

ROBERT MANNING, Esq., Secretary of the Massachusetts Horticultural Society.

GEORGE W. FOWLE, Esq., Treasurer of the Massachusetts Horticultural Society.

PHINEAS BROWN HOVEY, Esq., Member and one of the Founders of the Massachusetts Horticultural Society.

F. L. HARRIS, Esq., Member of the Massachusetts Horticultural Society.

JOHN C. HOVEY, Esq., Ex-Vice-president of the Massachusetts Horticultural Society.

CHARLES N. BRACKETT, Esq., Member of the Massachusetts Horticultural Society.

EDWARD L. BEARD, Esq., Member of the Massachusetts Horticultural Society.

JAMES COMELY, Esq., Member of the Massachusetts Horticultural Society.

AARON DAVIS CAPEN, Esq., Member of the Massachusetts Horticultural Society.

GEORGE HILL, Esq., Member of the Massachusetts Horticultural Society.

CHARLES H. BRECK, Esq., Member of the Massachusetts Horticultural Society.

LEANDER WETHERELL, Esq., Member of the Massachusetts Horticultural Society.

JOSEPH TAILBY, Esq., Member of the Massachusetts Horticultural Society.

HERMANN GRUNDEL, Esq., Member of the Massachusetts Horticultural Society.

CHARLES L. FOWLE, Esq., Member of the Massachusetts Horticultural Society.

EDWARD C. SPARHAWK, Esq., Member of the Massachusetts Horticultural Society.

C. A. READ, Esq., Member of the Massachusetts Horticultural Society.

WILLIAM T. HALL, Esq., Member of the Massachusetts Horticultural Society.

HUGH P. McNALLY, Esq., of the Sunday Courier.

HENRY O'MEARA, Esq., of the Boston Journal.

LYMAN WEEKS, Esq., of the Boston Post.

S. S. KINGDON, Esq., of the Daily Advertiser.

E. A. GROZIER, Esq., of the Boston Herald.

EDWIN L. HASKELL, Esq., of the Boston Star.

WILLIAM A. FORD, Esq., of the Saturday Evening Gazette.

MENU.

OYSTERS ON SHELL.

SOUP.

GREEN TURTLE.   CONSOMMÉ.

FISH.

CHICKEN HALIBUT, Hollandaise Sauce.

SMELTS, à la Tartare.

Cucumbers.   Tomatoes.

ENTRÉES.

LAMB CUTLETS, AUX CHAMPIGNONS.

CHICKEN CROQUETTE, à la Union.

RELEVE.

ROMAN PUNCH.

GAME.

ENGLISH SNIPE.   PHILADELPHIA SQUAB.

SWEETS.

CHARLOTTE RUSSE.   OMELETTE SOUFFLE.

WINE JELLY.   FROZEN PUDDING.

FRUITS.

PEACHES.   PEARS.   DELAWARE GRAPES.

HAMBURG GRAPES.   CONCORD GRAPES.

DRY FRUITS.

ICE CREAM.   SHERBET.

COFFEE.